Celebrity Cat Caper

A Klepto Cat Mystery

Patricia Fry

Matilija Press
PMB 123
323 E. Matilija St.,Ste 110
Ojai, CA 93023
www.matilijapress.com

Celebrity Cat Caper

A Klepto Cat Mystery
by Patricia Fry

ISBN 978-0-9908313-3-4

Cover Art: Bernadette E. Kazmarski
Cover layout: Dennis Mullican
Page layout: Dennis Mullican

Printed in U.S.A. by: Create Space

Other Novels by Patricia Fry

CATNAPPED
Cat-Eye Witness
Sleight of Paw
Undercover Cat
The Cat Colony Caper
The Corral Cat Caper
The Gallery Cat Caper
Mansion of Meows

Klepto Cat Mystery

Book Six: The Celebrity Cat Caper

By Patricia Fry

James took a step back, his eyes focused firmly on the heap in front of him. He stuffed his hands into his pockets to keep them from shaking and glanced over at his sidekick. "Is she dead?"

Just minutes earlier, the two men had stepped outside their travel trailer for a smoke. They'd barely had time to enjoy the rain-washed morning air when the Iveys' dog Lexie bounded down the porch steps. Savannah Ivey waved from the kitchen door, calling out, "Coffee will be ready in a minute."

When Lexie didn't return right away, Savannah walked out onto the wrap-around porch and peered along the south side of the house. "What does Lexie have?" she asked.

That's when James's sidekick, known to members of the film crew as Crank, slowly lifted his bulky frame from a lawn chair and ambled toward the barking dog. James, a wiry young man well into his twenties, reached Lexie's side first. Crank arrived seconds later. He stared down through bloodshot eyes under bushy white brows. Running one hand over his full beard, he muttered, "Well, hell." He nodded in response to James's question. "Yeah, she's dead, all right."

"What is it?" Savannah called from the porch, not wanting to walk across the wet grass in her slippers.

"Uh…ma'am," Crank said, "you'd better go get your husband…and call your dog, would you?"

"What's wrong?" Savannah asked.

Crank walked closer to where Savannah stood and spoke more softly, "There's been an accident, ma'am. Someone's been hurt. We need to call emergency."

Savannah, suddenly feeling her heart in her throat, glanced back at what appeared to be a pile of clothes draped across the rock edging next to the foundation of her home. She called Lexie and the two of them stepped into the kitchen. Savannah carefully lifted Lily out of the cradle swing and rushed to the bedroom with the baby in her arms. "Michael! Michael!" she called as she entered the room. When she saw him emerge from the bathroom, his face lathered with shaving cream, she could barely speak.

"What is it honey?" he asked, walking over to where she stood.

Finally, it came out. "Someone's been hurt." She hugged Lily to her and took a ragged breath before blurting, "Michael, I think someone's dead out there."

"What? Who?" he asked, his usual calm demeanor quickly unraveling.

"I don't know." She placed the baby in the middle of their bed and grabbed the house phone. "I have to call 9-1-1." After making the call, Savannah sat down next to Lily. She watched as Michael wiped his face dry and hastily pulled on a pair of jeans and a t-shirt. He grabbed his jacket off the back of a chair and headed out the bedroom door. "Oh Lily," Savannah said, lying down next to her, "what have I done, bringing all of these strangers into our peaceful life?" She closed her eyes and thought back to what had led to this decision.

***

It was several weeks earlier—the first day of Adam's spring vacation visit. Michael's son by a previous marriage would spend four days with the Iveys, and they'd made a lot of plans. Today there would be a picnic. Michael had gone to work at their veterinary clinic that Saturday morning as usual. Savannah was in the kitchen preparing for their guests when she heard Adam call out, "Savannah, the baby's crying."

She peered into the living room, wiped her hands, and promptly joined Adam and three-and-a-half-month-old Lily. "She looks happy to me," she said.

Adam glanced at his half-sister and said, "Oh. Well, she was making that crying face. I thought she was going to cry."

Savannah grinned at Adam. "Crying face?"

"Yeah, you know, when she scrunches up her face like this," he said, demonstrating the facial expression for Savannah. "Then she starts crying."

Savannah sat down next to the cradle swing and smoothed Lily's light-brown hair. The baby smiled and brought her stuffed calico-print cat up to her mouth with her chubby hands.

"Hey," Adam said, "cats aren't for eating, they're for petting." He took one of Lily's hands and moved it gently over the cat saying, "Pet it like this. See?"

Savannah smiled. "You are the best big brother ever, you know that, Adam? And you're a good teacher."

Adam looked down at Savannah's large grey-and-white cat and said solemnly, "Well, Rags isn't learning much from me."

"What are you trying to teach Rags?" she asked, her green eyes twinkling in amusement.

The boy's face lit up. "Tricks," he said excitedly. "I saw a cat on TV and he was doing tricks. They said only smart cats will do tricks, so I thought…"

Just then, they noticed Michael walking in through the front door. When he heard his son's statement, he laughed. "Well maybe old Rags here isn't so smart, huh?"

"Hi Dad," Adam said. "Are you through being an animal doctor today? Can we do something fun now?"

"You didn't have fun this morning?" Savannah asked, pretending to pout.

Adam blinked his eyes and said, "Yeah, you're fun, too. But Dad and I…we're going to do guy stuff today, right Dad?"

"Too many girls around here, huh, buddy?" Michael said with a laugh.

"Rags is a boy," Savannah said. "I guess that's why you were playing with him."

"Hey, what's this about teaching him tricks?" Michael asked as he sat down, removed his shoes and socks, and slipped on a pair of flip-flops.

"He saw a show where cats were doing tricks. He thinks Rags is smart enough to learn a few tricks," Savannah explained.

Michael picked up his daughter, kissed her on the cheek, and began making faces at her until she laughed. He placed the baby on his lap and smiled down at her. "Well, he is a smart cat," he told Adam, as he gently bounced Lily on his knee. "Maybe too smart."

"What do you mean, Dad?" he asked, standing and walking over to where Michael sat. He reached for one of Lily's hands and encouraged her to grip his finger.

"Well, Son, he might be too smart to want to do any silly tricks. He is so smart that he has decided he doesn't want to be a trick cat."

"Oh no." Adam pulled his hand from Lily's grip. "You can't eat my fingers," he said, giggling.

"What were you trying to get him to do?" Savannah asked, reaching over with a cloth diaper and wiping a little drool from Lily's chin.

Adam plopped down on his knees next to Rags, who had his front paws stretched out in front of him like an Egyptian cat statue. "Well, he likes to take things, right?"

Michael and Savannah both nodded.

"So I figured I could hide something and get him to find it—like hide-and-seek."

"If *you* hide, I'm sure he would find you," Savannah said. "But that's because he likes you. He would be motivated to find you."

Adam looked puzzled. "Motivated?"

"Yeah," Michael said, cuddling Lily close. "He would *want* to find you. He would be inspired to find you. He would have a reason to find you, because he wants to be with you."

"Oh," Adam said. He thought for a moment before suggesting, "So, I have to hide something he wants."

Michael nodded. "That's right."

"Like what?" he asked.

"Like a kitty treat, maybe," Savannah offered.

Adam jumped to his feet enthusiastically. "Yes, he would like that. Can I hide some of his treats and see if he'll find them?"

"Okay, but just a couple." Savannah pointed toward the dining room. "They're in the top drawer in the buffet."

"Hide your eyes, Rags," Adam said, upon returning with treats in his palm.

Instead, Rags began sniffing Adam's fisted hand.

"No, Rags, that's not how you play the game. You have to let me hide these. No, Rags." Adam raised his arm over his head and Rags stood on his hind feet, resting one paw on Adam's leg, and reaching up with the other paw as far as he could.

About then Lily started to fuss. She drew her hands up to her mouth.

"I think she's hungry," Michael said. "Is it time for her to eat?"

Savannah nodded. "Sure is. Here, I'll take her while you two see if you can train the cat." She chuckled. "Good luck with that." As she headed down the hallway toward the nursery, she called out, "There's lemonade in the fridge, if you guys get thirsty."

Twenty minutes later, Savannah returned carrying a baby monitor. "She's sound asleep," she said. "And our guests will arrive for the picnic in…" she looked at the large clock above the fireplace, "…about half an hour."

"Yay, a picnic. Do you mean outside?" Adam asked.

Savannah smiled. "Sure. It's a pretty day."

"Can Rags go out with us?"

"We'll see about that," she said. "Maybe while we're eating he should stay inside with Walter and Buffy. Lexie can come outside with us, though."

Adam looked over at the Afghan-mix dog as she lay in her bed near the staircase. "Dogs can go to picnics, but not cats?"

Michael reached out and tousled Adam's dark-brown hair. "Yeah, that's about the size of it, buddy."

"Isn't that 'criminating, Dad?" he asked.

Michael laughed. "Discrimination? Well, not really. And let me tell you why."

Adam stared up at his dad, waiting for an explanation. "Well, Dad?" he asked, his blue eyes wide with anticipation.

"Uh, well, cats are cats, and dogs are dogs."

"Yeah," Adam agreed, waiting for more.

Savannah smiled at her handsome husband and his nine-year-old clone. "Go on," she egged.

"That's it," he said with a shrug. "Different strokes for different folks."

"Huh?" Adam seemed confused.

"Well, cats and dogs are different, that's all. There are a lot of things cats can do that dogs can't, and a lot of things dogs can do that cats can't or don't want to do. They're different kinds of animals and they have to be treated differently…uh, for their own safety and comfort."

Adam thought about this for a moment. He looked down at Rags and then back up at his dad and said, "So, discrimination, right, Dad?"

Michael pursed his lips…chuckled. "Well, yeah, I guess it is a form of discrimination, isn't it, Son?" He squeezed the boy's shoulder and said, "But that's the way it is. No cats allowed at the picnic—at least while we're eating." He turned to Savannah. "So what needs to be done before guests arrive?"

"You two want a guy job?" she asked.

"Yeah," Adam said, with a little skip and jump.

"Okay, how about deciding where we should eat—on the porch or out on the lawn. Then you can set up the tables and chairs," she suggested.

"The grass," Adam said.

"Huh?" Michael asked.

"I want to eat on the grass. That's my vote."

Michael nodded and headed for the side kitchen door. "The grass it is," he said. "Let's go move the tables and chairs to the grass, shall we?"

***

The guest list was long by typical Ivey entertaining standards, but short when compared to that of their festive holiday party three months earlier. The picnic guest list included Savannah's Aunt Margaret and her husband, Max; their good friend, Iris and the man in her life, Detective Craig Sledge; Iris's grown son, Damon and his girlfriend Colbi (one of Savannah's best friends), both of whom were reporters for the local newspaper; and Savannah's sister, Brianna (a newly practicing doctor), and her beau, Bud, the newest veterinarian on staff at the Ivey Veterinary Clinic.

Once the guests had arrived and had been served their beverage of choice, Savannah, carrying the baby monitor in an apron pocket and a tray filled with hors d'oeurvres, ushered everyone outside.

"Who decorated the tables?" Iris asked, smiling over at Adam.

"Dad and me," he said. "I picked the flowers. They're…" He turned to Michael. "What are they, Dad?"

Michael shrugged. "I guess some kind of daisy."

"Daisies," Adam repeated.

"Well, good job," Iris said.

"Are there place cards?" Margaret asked.

Adam looked at her. "Huh?"

"Are we supposed to sit in any particular chair?" she explained.

"Uh…no, I don't think so," Adam said. "You can sit anywhere—only…" he grinned, "you'd better choose a lucky chair."

Margaret squinted at Adam with renewed interest. "Lucky chair?"

"Yeah," he said. "Some of the chairs are lucky and some aren't."

"Which ones are lucky?" she asked, her brown eyes dancing under thick dark-brown bangs.

"I can't tell you that, Aunt Maggie."

"So I have to take my chances, huh?" Margaret said. She examined the chairs, chose one, and sat down, glancing back at Adam for a response. Adam, however, was engaged in play with Lexie by then, on the other side of the expansive lawn.

Once everyone was seated, Adam ran over to where Michael sat and waited for the opportunity to speak. Finally, he saw an opening and jumped in. "Dad, can we do the prizes now?" he asked enthusiastically.

Michael, noticing that all the chairs were occupied, said, "I guess we can." He stood and said, "May I have your attention, please," and then he sat down.

That was Adam's cue. The boy said in a loud voice, "Okay, we're going to play a game and there are prizes."

Everyone smiled at Adam; there were a few comments.

"Cool," Max said.

Brianna exclaimed, "Prizes? Oh boy!"

"Pick me, pick me," Margaret begged.

Adam smiled and continued, "You win if you have a note that says 'prize.'"

Michael noticed that everyone seemed confused and he whispered, "Tell them where to look, Son."

"Oh, under your chair," Adam said. "Look on the bottom."

The guests stood and examined their chairs. Brianna was the first to shout, "I have one. Yay! I won a prize. What did I win, cutie?"

"I have one, too," Damon said, holding up the piece of paper he found taped to the bottom of his chair.

Adam smiled widely. "That's it. Only two prizes." He leaned toward Michael and asked, "Where are the prizes, Dad?"

"Where did you put them, buddy? In your room?"

"Oh, I remember. I'll go get them."

When he returned, he presented Brianna with a picture he had painted. "It's a horse," he said modestly.

"I can see that," Brianna said, pushing a dark brown curl from her forehead. "I love it. Thank you, buddy." She reached out and hugged the boy. "You know what? I like this so much I'm going to frame it and hang it in my office."

"Your doctor's office?" he asked.

"Yes, right in the waiting room."

"Awesome," Adam said, smiling.

"But there's something missing here," Brianna said.

Adam's smile faded. "What?" he asked hesitantly.

"The artist's signature," she said. "Would you sign it for me?"

Adam looked at Michael, his eyes wide, and then back at the painting. "Uh, yeah. I guess," he said. "I'll go get a pen."

"Here's one," Bud offered.

"Thanks," Adam said, taking the pen and carefully writing his name at the bottom of the painting.

"Way cool," Brianna said. "Thanks."

Adam was still smiling shyly when he walked over to Damon, a gift bag in his hand. "It's an eraser. I won it at school."

"All right!" Damon said. "How'd you win it?"

"I spelled a bunch of words right."

Damon displayed his sideways grin and winked. "So since you can spell, you don't need an eraser anymore, huh?"

Adam stared down at his feet. Before he could respond, Damon patted the boy on the back. "Thanks Adam. I can really use this. Good prize."

"Hey, who wants to help me cook the hamburgers?" Michael asked.

"I do, I do," Adam said, following his dad toward the house. "Can I flip them with your big turner-over thing?" he asked as they entered the kitchen.

Michael chuckled. "Flip them? They aren't pancakes, you know," he said as he pulled a tray of burger patties out of the refrigerator.

Adam, eyes downward, said, "Yeah, I know. Well, can I turn them?"

Michael studied his son for a moment and said, "We'll see. Maybe we can give it a try. You're probably big enough to handle that job."

Adam jumped up and down a couple of times. "Yay!"

"Only if you drop one, it's yours," Michael said with a grin.

Adam frowned. "Well, how would I know that the one I dropped is mine?"

Michael laughed. "If you drop one, that one is yours. That's how you'll know."

Adam thought about that for a moment and then he flashed his dad a wide smile and said, "Then I guess I won't drop any."

Michael laughed out loud and tousled his son's hair.

Within forty minutes, the meal was served. "Good job on the hamburgers, Adam," Max said after taking a couple of bites.

"Thanks," the boy responded. "I turned some of them over and didn't drop any." He took a bite of his burger, swallowed, and added, "I helped Dad make the sauce, too. It's a barbecue sauce. I squeezed the ketchup and mustard…oh, and the honey…"

Max set his burger down on his plate. "Impressive. Do you think you'd like to be a chef someday?" he asked.

Adam scrunched up his face. "A chef?"

"Yeah, a cook. You could prepare meals for the president."

The boy's eyes widened. "Of the United States?"

"Sure, why not?" Max said. "Or you could open your own restaurant," he suggested.

Margaret jumped into the conversation. She patted her husband's arm and said to Adam, "Max could be your mentor. You know, he used to be a chef."

"You did?" Adam said. "Did you cook for the president?"

Max laughed. "No. I was chef at restaurants in Chicago," he responded.

Adam looked at Max as if seeing him for the first time. "Cool. Do you cook for your cats?" he asked.

"Sure do," he said. "Some of the cats that come into the shelter need a special diet. So I cook chicken for them."

"Max, your beans are to die for," Iris said. "What makes them so delicious?" she asked.

He narrowed his lips in contemplation. "I guess it's a combination of things." He looked at Iris. "You know, cooking is a science or an art—however you want to look at it. It takes practice to learn what pairs well together, how much of it to use, and all."

"He's like a mad scientist in the kitchen," Margaret said with a chuckle.

"I like science," Adam offered. "And I like art. I guess I could be a…cook." He took a sip of lemonade and then said, "Hey, I could be on the cooking channel."

Michael laughed. "He's our budding celebrity," he said. He leaned toward the group as if sharing a secret. "You know, he's thinking about joining the circus."

"The circus?" Brianna asked. "Are you serious?"

"Yes," Savannah said. "With Rags."

"Oh, you're going to be a lion tamer, huh?" Bud asked with a chuckle.

Adam glanced up at everyone and took another bite of his burger. "No," he said. "Rags isn't a lion. He does cat tricks."

Just then, Savannah jumped up from her chair and darted toward the house. "The baby's awake," she said over her shoulder.

Colbi stood and rushed to catch up with Savannah's long strides. "Can I help?"

As they entered the kitchen, Savannah saw their little Himalayan-mix cat walking toward them. "Oh, hi there, Buffy. Is our girl awake?" She then addressed Colbi, "There's our best baby monitor."

Colbi seemed confused. She pushed her soft side bangs off her forehead and asked, "Where?"

"Right there," Savannah said, pointing at the cat. "Buffy comes to tell us when Lily wakes up."

"Awww, how cute is that?" she said bending down and ruffling the cat's lush fur.

Once the two women had returned to the picnic, baby Lily cuddled in Colbi's arms, Adam asked his dad for permission to bring Rags out to perform tricks for their guests.

"Let's clear the table first, shall we?" Savannah suggested. Margaret, Iris, and Brianna stood and began helping Savannah and Michael with the task.

"Now, Dad?" Adam pestered, once coffee and cherry cobbler had been served.

"Okay, Son. Go get our entertainment."

When the boy returned with the large grey-and-white cat in a harness attached to a long tether, Michael stood and asked for everyone's attention.

"Are we going to have an announcement?" Margaret asked. She glanced expectantly at Colbi and Damon, and then at Brianna and Bud. "Is someone getting married?"

Once Margaret had duly embarrassed both couples, she smiled brightly and said more reverently, "Well, I hope you don't wait too long."

"No one's getting married," Michael said. He then added, "…that I know of." He chuckled and ran his hand through his straight dark-brown hair. "We have some entertainment this afternoon." He winked at Adam and addressed the crowd. "Can we have a drum roll, please?"

As the guests tapped their fingers on the tables, Adam said, "Dad, that's going to scare Rags." He waved his hand. "Stop, you're scaring my trick cat."

The boy, ignoring the muffled laughter, patted Michael on the arm and said, "Okay, now introduce us, Dad."

Michael bellowed, "Please welcome into the ring, Adam and his circus cat, Raaaaaaaags."

Adam smiled shyly as the captive audience exploded into exuberant applause. Then he addressed Michael. “Okay. First, Dad, hold him and don’t let him peek.”

Michael placed the cat on his lap and faced him in the opposite direction Adam had walked. In the meantime, the boy opened a packet of kitty treats and began placing them in strategic spots throughout the area. He put one in the cuff of Max’s slacks, balanced one on the leather bow on Iris’s turquoise designer shoes, and dropped a couple at the base of Lily’s baby swing. He looked around and asked, “Where else can I hide these?”

“How about here on my lap,” Colbi said. “Do you think he’ll jump up in my lap for a treat?”

Adam nodded. “Um, maybe.”

She took a cat treat from Adam and tucked it into a fold of her full skirt.

“Here, put one on my cap,” Damon suggested, motioning toward the baseball cap lying on the grass under his chair.

“That’s probably enough, Adam, don’t you think?” Savannah suggested.

The boy nodded. “Okay, now let’s see if you can find the treats, trick cat,” Adam said, taking the leash in his hand as Michael set the large cat on the ground. “Find the treats!” Adam commanded, urging the cat along.

Suddenly Lexie, who had been lying next to Savannah, raised her head and sniffed the air. She stood and started to move toward Adam, when Savannah caught her by the collar and said, “No, Lexie. You stay put. This is a cat circus; no dogs allowed.”

Adam chuckled. “That’s right, no dogs allowed.”

In the meantime, Rags began leading Adam away from the group and across the lawn toward a flowerbed. Craig spoke up. “Hey big boy, wrong direction.”

Brianna called out, “Come over here, kitty, kitty.”

“That’s where he likes to chase butterflies,” Savannah explained.

Margaret grinned. “He wants a butterfly treat.”

Adam continued tugging on the leash, saying, “No, Rags. Come this way. Your treats are over here.”

Rags resisted for a moment and then decided to trot along next to Adam back to the group. The cat walked over near Iris, peered up at her, and took a few more steps toward her. Suddenly, something caught his attention. He began sniffing the air. The scent seemed to direct him toward the ground. He sniffed around Iris’s feet and then he found it—a treat sitting on one of her shoes. He reached out with one paw and attempted to grasp the round treat. Instead, it fell into the thick grass. Adam felt around among the blades, picked up the treat, and fed it to Rags. “Good boy,” he said with a wide smile.

The cat looked up at Iris. *Meow*.

“That’s all I have,” she said, opening her palms toward him.

Everyone applauded and cheered. Adam grinned from ear to ear.

Just then, Max reached one hand down and wriggled his fingers to attract the cat’s attention. Rags saw this and promptly trotted in his direction. Max brought his hands back up to his lap and Rags promptly jumped up, resting his front paws on the man’s knee. When Max dropped one hand toward the ground again, Rags followed it with his eyes. He sniffed Max’s hand and then he seemed to catch a whiff of something else. It didn't take him long to locate the treat and dig it out of Max's pants cuff.

The group burst into applause again.

Rags ran his pink tongue around the outside of his mouth while Adam petted and praised the cat. "There are three more, Rags. Can you find them?" he said. He tugged on the leash, leading the cat to the other side of the table. When they neared where Colbi sat, Adam stopped and relaxed his grip on the leash.

Colbi smiled down at the cat. "Hi there, Rags. Want a treat? Huh?" she said while lightly tapping one hand against her thigh.

Rags hopped up onto her lap with his front paws and quickly found the treat.

There was more applause and a few cheers.

"Two more," Adam announced, as he walked toward Savannah and baby Lily. It didn't take long for Rags to discover the treats at the base of the baby swing. After swallowing them, he stood up with his paws on the swing and began sniffing Lily.

At the same time, Adam looked around. "I forgot where the other one is," he admitted.

Just then, Rags jumped down and walked away from Adam. Feeling the tug on the leash, the boy followed the cat to where Damon sat and watched as he began foraging around Damon's feet. Within a few seconds, Rags was under the chair retrieving the treat Adam had left on Damon's cap.

"You've done a good job of training him," Margaret said. "Or did he train you to give him those treats?"

At the same time, Colbi asked Savannah, "Have you ever thought about using him as a therapy cat?"

"Not really," Savannah said. "Do you mean take him around to visit old folks in nursing homes?"

"Yeah, or, he could help kids learn to read."

Savannah looked at Colbi quizzically, her blond ponytail brushing across one shoulder.

Colbi explained, "I'm preparing a news story on illiteracy and children's reading programs. Some of the programs involve animals—you know, cats and dogs, mostly—and an occasional pony, hamster, guinea pig…"

Margaret leaned forward in her chair. "I've heard of programs where special-needs kids are exposed to shelter animals—animals have a calming effect on them," she said. "But how do animals help kids learn to read?"

"Yeah, my friend Bonnie has a riding program at her stable for children with disabilities," Savannah said. "But I can't imagine how horses or cats could help kids read. How does that work?" she asked, reaching over and caressing one of baby Lily's feet as Brianna lifted the baby onto her lap.

"Well, what slow learners and poor readers need is more practice. Teachers don't have time to work with these kids. Some children don't do well reading in front of their classmates anyway, because they have such low self-esteem. Their parents are stressed to the limit or are disinterested—heck, some of them don't even speak English. So they don't encourage the children to read the books they get at school. And parents can be critical, which feeds the student's general lack of confidence. You can see how, for some children, reading just makes them feel like a failure."

Briana gazed across at Colbi. "So what difference can an animal make?" she asked.

"They're good listeners. They don't judge. They give these students the opportunity to practice reading in a non-threatening environment. I'm telling you, the statistics gathered on some of these programs are quite remarkable."

Damon leaned into the conversation. "Being around animals is thought to lower blood pressure, so there's also the therapeutic value of the programs. It's a nice environment for kids to learn in and they gain some confidence in their skills."

"So, you think Rags would be a good listener?" Savannah asked, looking from Damon to Colbi.

"Yeah, what if he doesn't like the story?" Margaret joked.

"Wow," Craig said, "I didn't know animals could be so important."

Michael laughed. "How did you miss that memo after hanging around this bunch for the past few years, Craig?"

"Yeah," Brianna said, "three veterinarians, three cat-rescue people, and almost all of us own pets. Bud has lots of all kinds of critters out at his place."

Before Craig could respond, Iris fixed her eyes harshly on his and asked, "Don't you think Willie's important?"

He cleared his throat before speaking. "Sure, I like your kids' dog. He's a good dog. I'm just saying, I didn't know that you could give animals—especially cats—a job like that."

Savannah sat straighter in her chair. "Craig, what about the work Rags has done for you? That was important, wasn't it? I mean he has helped you solve some serious crimes."

"Okay, you've got me," Craig said. "I have to admit, I've gained a whole lot more respect for cats since I met Rags."

Margaret looked across the table at Damon. She smiled. "I hear you like cats now, too."

Damon smoothed his short-cropped curly red hair with one hand. "Yeah, cats—at least some cats—are pretty awesome creatures." He pointed to Rags. "That one saved my life."

Craig reached over and squeezed the younger man's shoulder affectionately.

"Rags saved your life?" Adam asked from where he and the cat were playing nearby. "How'd he do that?"

Damon wasn't sure how to respond. He didn't want to tell the boy that he'd been a drug addict and committed a crime and that, because Rags identified him as an accessory to murder, he went to prison. He didn't think the child would understand how difficult it had been to get off drugs, but that with Craig's support and his own determination, he'd managed to come clean and change his life. Finally, he turned toward the boy and said, "Well, Adam, I was sick and needed help getting well. Rags made sure I got the help I needed."

"Oh," Adam said before jumping up and following Rags who had sprinted across the lawn.

Colbi reached over and patted Damon's leg. "I love you," she mouthed silently. He leaned in and kissed her.

Iris smiled at her son and Colbi. She then asked, "Do we have any reading programs here in Hammond like the one you mentioned?"

Colbi pushed one side of her long brown hair behind one ear. "No, not at this time. Maybe it would be a good project for the Hammond Cat Alliance to initiate. There might be others in the group with cats that would be good candidates."

"Can you get me some information about reading programs with animals?" Savannah asked.

"I'd be interested in being a part of that committee, if one develops," Iris said, tugging lightly at the hem of her fitted turquoise crop-top.

"Super," Savannah said. "Let's look into it. Rags could use some extracurricular activities now that he's between sleuth jobs." She thought for a moment and then suggested, "Shall we start with the library? Maybe the librarian can help us coordinate something."

"Who is librarian now that poor Leslie Sparks went crazy?" Margaret asked.

No one responded for a few seconds and then Iris spoke, "I didn't know there was a new librarian; what happened to Leslie?"

"I thought you'd be one of the first to hear, since you work at the gossip center of town," Margaret said.

Iris abruptly straightened her posture. "The operative word here is *work*, Maggie. I don't sit around all day at the diner listening to the tittle-tattle. I'm working." She knitted her brows. "Where is Leslie, anyway? I haven't seen her around in ages."

"It was kept kind of hush-hush, actually." Margaret looked around to make sure everyone was listening and then she said quietly, "She's in an institution somewhere. Had a breakdown."

"That pretty thing?" Iris said. "What could go so wrong in her life? She had it all, didn't she?"

"So it seemed." Margaret scanned the area for Adam. When she saw him racing around in the orchard with Lexie, out of earshot, she continued, "But when her husband disappeared under mysterious circumstances three or four years ago, she lost it…couldn't cope, I guess. Ended up over in Straley at the mental hospital."

"I remember that case," Craig said. "Still unsolved. I think about it once in a while. I half expect Chris Sparks to show up someday out of the blue."

"You don't think he's dead?" Max asked.

Craig shook his head. "Don't know. He left a note saying he was leaving town for good."

"In his handwriting?" Colbi asked.

"No, it was typed. We checked—it came from his home computer."

"So who's the librarian now?" Savannah asked.

"Her name is Glenda Cathcart," Damon said. "I met her when I was digging up stuff about the old Fischer building a few months ago for a newspaper article."

"Well, I might just make an appointment with Ms. Cathcart and see if I can get Rags a job," Savannah said. She looked at Iris. "I'll let you know what I find out."

Chapter 2

The following Monday afternoon, Savannah pulled up in front of Iris's house. "Where's Lily?" Iris asked upon climbing into the car.

"Michael worked half day so he can spend more time with Adam while he's here. She's hanging out with the guys."

Iris's smile widened. "How is that adorable baby?" she asked.

"Great. Just great. If I'd known how special being a mom is, I'd have…"

"You'd have what?" Iris asked, smirking at her friend.

"Oh, I don't know—maybe let things play out just the way they did; otherwise, I might have ended up with a bratty Brian or a crabby Clara. We waited just the right amount of time to have adorable, sweet Lily. What a gift she is," Savannah said with a sigh.

"Yeah, you lucked out. She's precious," Iris said. "By the way, when can Craig and I babysit?"

"Uh, well, gosh, Michael and I don't go out much unless we take her with us." She hesitated. "But she could come over for a playdate sometime, if you want."

"That would be great. Let me find out when Craig will be at my house and we'll make a plan—for sure."

"You'll probably have your son and his girlfriend over there, too. They sure are in love with our baby, aren't they?"

"Yes, Damon cracks me up the way he just melts when he sees Lily—or Colbi's kitty, Dolly…"

"Or Colbi…" Savannah, said laughing.

Iris laughed as well. "Yeah, he does love that girl."

"And I think the feeling's mutual."

"Savannah, I can't tell you how…" Iris's voice cracked and she paused before continuing.

"I know, Iris. It must be a wonderful feeling to see him doing so well and being so happy after having it so rough there for a while."

"I bless Craig every day for the time he spent helping Damon to find himself, to discover his passion, and get off those horrible drugs." Iris turned to face Savannah. "That's one reason why I want to be involved in the reading program."

"Oh? How's that?"

"Well, I have to think that if Damon had something like that when he was young, maybe, just maybe, he wouldn't have gone down the wrong path. I'd love to do something to help other kids make good decisions. Drugs are the devil's doing—I'm sure of it—and we must do what we can to deter impressionable kids, who don't yet have goals and a strong set of values, from taking a wrong turn."

Savannah glanced at her friend and then back at the road. "Noble, Iris."

"What?"

"That's noble of you. I honor you for paying it forward."

"Any mother would do the same, if presented with the opportunity."

Savannah parked her SUV outside the Hammond library just before two that afternoon. "Hey, wait for me, girl," Iris said as Savannah took the front steps at a fast pace. "Where's the fire?"

"Oh, sorry, you've got those high heels on—no wonder you're lagging."

"And I have a few years on you, too, remember?"

"Yeah, I do keep forgetting that, Grandma," Savannah said teasingly.

“I’m still bigger than you—well, taller,” Iris snapped.

“By half an inch,” Savannah said. “But you must stand, what, six-foot-two in those monster shoes you’re wearing?”

Iris shook her head. “Not quite.”

Savannah opened the door at the top of the stairs and the two of them walked up to the front desk.

“Ms. Cathcart, please?” Savannah said in a hushed tone.

“I’m Glenda Cathcart. You must be Savannah Ivey, here to talk about a reading program.”

“Yes, and this is Iris Clampton.”

Glenda nodded and smiled. “Come on; we can talk in here,” she said as she led the two women past the reference section and into her small office.

Forty-five minutes later, the first stage of the proposed program was set. The librarian would send notices to all local grammar schools in order to find out if there was any interest, and Savannah and Iris would contact Alliance members to locate those with cats that might be calm enough to participate in a reading program. Savannah would also go into the schools by invitation to share what she had recently learned about the success of reading programs involving animals.

“Do you have the time to visit all the schools like that?” Iris asked as Savannah drove her home. “I’d help, but since I don’t even have a cat…”

“I doubt there will be much call for our visits. But I’m sure I can get a few others to help—Colbi’s kitten Dolly might be a good candidate for the program, and my sister’s kitten Frankie. Auntie has a few cats at her place that would qualify, too”

“Don’t she and Max rescue wild cats?” Iris asked.

"Yes, feral and also domesticated strays—abandoned cats. They get some gentle ones, too, and they have some quiet, calm cats of their own."

"Oh that's right. Layla is a calm cat. Will you take Buffy to help out?" Iris asked. "She should be perfect for the job. She loves to lap-sit."

Savannah thought for a moment and said, "She's kind of an old lady and doesn't like to step outside her comfort zone. I'm not sure how she'd do. It might be a bit overwhelming for Buffy." She glanced over at Iris. "We want both the cats and the kids to have a good experience."

"Makes sense," Iris said. She smiled. "I just love that fluffy little cat."

"More than Rags?" Savannah teased.

Iris smirked and rolled her eyes. "What's to love about a thief?" She reached out and touched Savannah's arm. "I'd take Buffy in a heartbeat, but I'm not sure I could handle all of the excitement that comes with your klepto cat."

Savannah laughed. "Granted, he is a handful. There's never a dull moment with Rags around."

Savannah pulled into Iris's driveway, and the attractive redhead stepped out of the car. She turned and waved, calling out, "Take care, girlfriend."

"Hey," Savannah shouted, "let me know when you want a playdate with Lily. Maybe Michael and I'll go to a movie or something."

"Sure will," Iris said. She threw a kiss and walked up the two steps into her house.

***

The following day, Michael, Savannah, and Lily were on their way back from taking Adam home. "She still snoozing?" Michael asked.

Savannah looked at the baby, smiled, and said, "Yup. Your driving puts her to sleep."

Michael glanced at Savannah through the rearview mirror. "I miss having you in the front seat with me."

"Well, I just feel better being able to see her in case there's a problem or she wakes up frightened or something. I hate that they make you face the baby backward in the backseat now. There's no way parents driving the car can keep an eye on their infant."

"I know. But we can turn her around when she's what—a year?"

"Yes, a year old and weighing twenty pounds, although longer is better, they say."

Michael started chuckling.

"What's so funny?" she asked.

"Oh just thinking about Adam and his plan to start a reading program for kids and cats in his school."

"He might just pull it off," Savannah said. "He's one smart cookie."

"He wants to take Tiger to his classroom."

"His kitty seems a little high-strung to be a therapy cat, don't you think?"

"Probably so," he said with a laugh. "He might have his hands full taking Tiger to school." He glanced back at Savannah again and asked, "So how's your program coming along?"

"Good," she said. "Colbi wants to try working with Dolly. Oh, remember Janice Tuttle—the gal with the angoras? She has one that she's sure would be a wonderful listener for a child. And Auntie wants to audition Layla for the program."

"Oh, so the cats will be auditioning, will they?"

"Can't allow any wild cats or scaredy-cats," she said in a serious tone. Savannah jumped and reached into her pocket. "Oh, that's my phone." She looked at the screen. "I don't recognize the number." Into the phone, she said, "Hello?"

Several minutes later, Savannah ended the call and dropped the phone on her lap.

"Who was it?" Michael asked, frowning into the rearview mirror.

"Well," Savannah said, "remember at our Christmas party when Craig got a call from a reporter who wanted to do a story about Rags?"

"Yeah, and he did that little write-up," Michael recalled.

"You mean that article written tongue-in-cheek by that rather skeptical reporter?"

Michael nodded. "That's the one."

"Well, that night, Craig said the guy had mentioned doing a film. This call was from a documentary filmmaker wanting to meet with us."

"Really!?" Michael said. "When?"

"A preliminary meeting next week—he thought maybe Monday or Tuesday evening, and he wants to start filming as early as April tenth."

Michael made quick and fleeting eye-contact with Savannah. "What do you think?"

"Well, you heard me. I said I'd talk it over with you and call him back." She looked down at Lily and said, "I don't know, Michael. What will it mean? How intrusive will this be into our lives? What demands will be put on us? How will it affect Rags—and the other animals? How will it benefit our family, if at all?"

Michael was silent for a moment and then he said, "I guess that's why we would have a preliminary meeting—to get answers to all of that, right? And as far as benefits, maybe you can tie in your work with children and get some publicity for your reading project."

Savannah nodded. She ran her finger over Lily's pudgy little hand. "I guess so." She took a deep breath. "So when do you want to meet?"

***

It had been raining steadily all day when Rob Willoughby arrived at the Iveys' home the following Monday evening. After introductions, Savannah excused herself and carried Lily off to the nursery.

"He's quite a handsome devil," Rob said, looking at the large grey-and-white cat who sat on the coffee table staring at him through clear green eyes. "Okay if I pet him?"

Michael smiled. "Sure. He usually likes a good scratch on the head or behind the ear."

"Is that how you pet a cat?" he asked, reaching out toward Rags.

When Rags turned to sniff his hand, Rob pulled it back. "Does he want to bite me?" he asked.

"No, he wants to get to know you by your scent. He might also find out what you had for dinner, what kind of soap you use, whether or not you petted any other animals before coming here…" Michael explained with a laugh.

Rob raised his eyebrows. "Really!? That's a lot of information—and to think…not one word of it is spoken." He reached out toward the cat again and let him sniff his fingers. Rags stood and pushed his head against Rob's hand. "What's he doing now?" he asked, holding his hand still.

"He's putting his scent on you," Michael said. "Now if you pet another animal, the animal will smell Rags's scent. It's his way of…dibsing you."

"Dibsing him?" Savannah said as she entered the room, carrying the baby monitor.

"Yeah, you know, 'dibs, he's mine,'" Michael explained.

Both Rob and Savannah laughed. She said, "Yeah, cats can be possessive beings."

"Territorial," Michael added.

Rob pushed one side of his unkempt shoulder-length brown hair away from his face. "So now, I'm his territory?" he asked.

Savannah noticed that Rags was still staring at the lanky man. "I think so," she said. She then announced, "Baby's asleep. All is calm. Would you like something to drink, Rob? We have bottles of water, coffee, soda, apple juice, tea…"

"After driving in all that rain tonight to get here, hot coffee sounds good, if you don't mind."

Michael stood. "I'll get it," he said as he headed toward the kitchen. He stopped and asked, "Cream or sugar?"

"Black," Rob said. "Thanks." Once Michael had disappeared into the kitchen, Rob said, "So, Mrs. Ivey…"

"Savannah," she corrected.

"Okay, Savannah…" He paused before asking, "Are you from Georgia?"

She shook her head. "No. My folks just liked the 'anna' names. My sister is Brianna. I suppose if they'd had more daughters, they would have been Hannah, PollyAnna, Susanna, RoseAnna…and who knows what they would have named a boy."

Rob laughed. "It's a pretty name. Better than Zamir."

"Zamir?" she asked.

"My middle name—well one of them. I'm Robert Zamir DeCloud Willoughby."

"Sounds…important," Savannah said.

He smirked. "Sounds like a bad committee decision."

"So did a committee name you?" she asked. "I mean, was there input by several family members?"

"Yeah, as a matter of fact. My mom, dad, older sister, grandfather, and an uncle. That uncle always called me 'Spider.'"

Savannah laughed. "So his choice of names didn't get a vote; is that it?"

"That's right," he said, joining her in laughter. He then turned somber. "But that was a long time ago. Everyone's gone now. I lost most of my family before I entered high school. Just my sister and I are left."

"Do you have your own family?" Savannah asked.

"No, never did marry." Rob was quiet for a moment. "I'm forty-nine now, and that's something I regret."

Michael walked into the room with two cups of coffee. "I didn't think you wanted coffee tonight, hon. What can I get you to drink?"

"A glass of herbal iced tea sounds good, if you don't mind."

"Coming right up."

Savannah turned her attention back to their guest. "So tell me about the work you do and how you think our cat might fit into the scheme of things."

Rob prepared to speak, when Savannah said, "Oh, sorry, let's wait until Michael returns, if you don't mind. I want him in on all of this."

"Do I have to start over with my name?" he asked, a twinkle in his hazel eyes.

She shook her head. "Naw. Probably not necessary."

When Michael returned with Savannah's tea, she said, "Thank you, hon. Rob was just going to explain how he envisions working with Rags."

An hour and a half later, Michael said, "Well, you've given us a lot to think about, Rob. And that's just what Savannah and I'll do over the next few days, if you don't mind. We have your number; we'll call you, say, by Friday?"

"Sure," he said with a shrug. "And let me know if you have any questions, will you?"

"Are you staying over in town?" Savannah asked as Rob began to put on his jacket.

"Yeah. I have friends in the area. I'll head home in a few days."

"Uh-oh. Wait, Rob. Is that yours?" Michael asked.

The visitor furrowed his brow. "What?"

"Appears to be a plane ticket. Hey, Rags, come here with that. Darn cat," Michael said as he took off up the stairs after the streak of grey-and-white fur.

Savannah grimaced. "I'm sorry," she said. "I hope it isn't anything important."

"Um, well…" he said as he patted his jacket pockets. I did have an airline ticket. It doesn't seem to be here. So what's the deal? He steals?"

"Yes, big time. It's one of his…"

"Charms?" Rob offered.

"Charms? Well, that depends…"

"On whether you're the victim, I suppose," Rob said with a wide grin.

"Right." Savannah turned to face Rob. "Well, this is what you wanted to see…Rags's methods of helping to solve crimes."

"Only sometimes, he's the one committing the crime, right?"

Savannah nodded—a hint of exasperation evident on her pretty face. "So what did he have?" she asked when she saw Michael heading back down the stairs.

He held a packet out toward Rob. "Is this yours?"

After quickly examining it, Rob said, "Well, I'll be. That knucklehead pulled this right out of my pocket. Thanks, Michael, for retrieving it; otherwise I would have been in a world of hurt. Yes, it's an airline ticket. I bought it for my sister as a birthday gift, so she can visit her only grandson in Texas next week. He's almost a year old and she's never seen him." He looked down at the ticket in his hand, shook his head, and said, "Someone had better teach that cat the difference between private property and clues to a crime."

Michael laughed. "You've never been owned by a cat, have you, Rob?"

He shook his head.

"Well, you have a lot to learn about the feline species." Michael grinned. "I can tell you this: if we do this documentary, you'll walk away either disliking cats or completely enthralled with them."

Once the Iveys had bid their guest farewell, closed the door, and turned off the lights, they headed down the hallway toward the nursery. "Well, what do you think? Do we want to get involved in the film industry?" Michael asked.

Without answering, Savannah stepped into the nursery, adjusted the blanket over their baby, and bent down and kissed her on the forehead. Michael smiled at the sleeping infant. "She is so beautiful," he whispered, putting one arm around Savannah and squeezing her to him, "like her mama."

Before stepping out of the room, Savannah knelt down and affectionately petted Buffy, who was curled up in her pink canopy bed in a corner of the nursery. "You watch over our girl, will you,

Buffy?" Savannah said. She looked up at Michael. "Isn't it uncanny how much she wants to be with Lily?" She shook her head. "I wasn't for having cats in this room at all, but this little dear insisted, didn't she?"

Michael laughed. "Yeah, she wouldn't budge off the changing table until we moved her bed in here."

"Oh, hi Rags," Savannah said. "Look honey, Rags is giving Buffy a goodnight kiss."

Once they were in their own bedroom next door, baby monitor set up on the bedside table, Savannah said, "Well, Michael, it sounds like it could be kind of fun to go through with the documentary. Like you said, it would shine some light on our reading program. If the program proves to be successful, it would be wonderful to get the publicity and, perhaps, inspire other school districts and libraries to do something similar. I think fighting illiteracy is important."

"I can't argue with that," Michael said, "… but…"

Savannah interrupted. "Did you hear the figure Rob threw out? Like Craig said several months ago, the money would help put our kids through college."

"Yeah, but…" he said.

"What's your but, Michael?" she asked, tilting her head, her blond hair flaring over one shoulder.

"My but is, as you brought up a couple of days ago, do we want to invite the chaos into our home?"

"You heard Rob; it may be only a matter of a few days of filming. They get footage they think they can use and then do splicing and stuff in the studio."

"How many people would be coming here?" he asked.

"As I understand it, he would direct the film, there would be videographers, and an assistant to Rob—assistant producer, I guess—clean-up people…so what's that, maybe a half dozen?" Savannah took in a deep breath. "Yeah, kind of a lot of people, but we have a lot of room. Since they're used to doing this sort of thing, it might not be too chaotic."

"Lights out?" Michael asked after sliding into bed next to his wife.

"Yeah, I'm ready," she said. She ran her hand over Rags, who was sitting next to her pillow. "Are you ready, Mr. Rags?"

Prrrrt.

As the room went dark, Savannah said, "It might be a kind of fun adventure. Maybe Adam would like to come and watch the filming." She was quiet for a moment and then she said, "I think I'd like to do it. How do you feel, Michael?"

"Kind of lukewarm at the moment. But if it's something you want to do, I can't think of too many reasons why not."

***

"So what are you two doing today?" Michael asked as he walked out of the bathroom into their bedroom the following morning.

Savannah had just changed Lily's diaper and was sitting next to her on their king-size bed. "I'm meeting with the librarian to talk about our reading program. She's heard back from some of the schools and is eager to put a plan into motion."

"So you and Lily will be out running around, huh?"

"No, Glenda's coming here for tea this afternoon. Lily should be napping about then. She's on a pretty good schedule now."

Michael smiled down at their daughter. "And she's such a happy baby, so contented. Are all babies like that?"

"I don't think so—not from what I hear. I think we're lucky."

"Boy *are* we." Michael was silent. He sat down on the other side of Lily and said, "I wonder sometimes what kind of baby Adam was. Since I didn't meet him until he was already eight years old, I missed all of his infant and toddler years."

"I'll bet he was a model child," Savannah said with a smile. She reached out and smoothed her hand over her husband's hair.

"It's easy to imagine that he was. He's such a…" he started to choke up. "He's just a great kid. I'm so glad Marci finally told me about him and that we can spend time with him. But now that we have Lily, I do wonder about…"

"Honey, I think we ought to just enjoy the boy we know and not let regret enter into our relationship with him or with Marci and Eric. We couldn't ask for a more charming, fun, interesting, bright boy or a better relationship with his other parents. I'd say we should cherish what we have."

Michael took a deep breath. "You're right, of course. Thank you," he said, kissing her. He then lifted Lily's little shirt and blew raspberries on her belly. She kicked her legs and giggled out loud. Michael and Savannah laughed. He did it again and Lily giggled again.

Savannah stood, grabbed her cell phone off the nightstand, and started recording the play session, laughing so hard she had trouble holding the phone still. "Oh, I have to send this to my mom," she said after viewing the video. She plopped down on the bed and said, "I sure miss Mom being here to watch her grow and change and learn."

"I know you do. Let's make it a point to have her visit more often. She hasn't been here since Lily was born, has she?"

"No. She's due." Savannah smiled. "She does love seeing the videos and pictures I send though, and we use your computer camera sometimes to visit. You knew I sent her a camera for her computer, didn't you?"

Michael nodded while picking up Lily. He held her close. "Family is sure important, isn't it?" He looked over at Savannah. "I wish my parents were here. They died too young to know either of their grandchildren, or you. They would have loved you."

***

Later that morning, Savannah had finished bathing and feeding Lily. She held the baby in her arms while reading a nursery rhyme out loud.

Rap-rap. "Vannie?"

"Come in, Auntie—door's open."

Margaret pushed her way in, placed her hands on her ample hips, and scolded, "What have I told you about leaving your door unlocked, young lady?"

"I knew you were coming."

"Okay, then," she said, relaxing her stance. She rushed toward Savannah. "Awww, look how precious. You're reading to her?"

"Yes, watch this." Savannah began to read and baby Lily stared up at her as if she were hanging on every word.

"Pshaw! *Old King Cole*?" Margaret said. "How about the *Three Little Kittens*?"

"Oh, she likes that one, too, and *There Was a Crooked Man*. She's not discriminating. She's a literary little thing."

"Let me hold her—go get me a cup of that yummy herbal tea you make."

"Okay," Savannah said, handing the baby over.

"Got any muffins or brownies or cookies?"

"As a matter of fact, peach pie. Interested?"

"Yeowza!" Margaret said. She followed Savannah into the kitchen with Lily in her arms."So tell me about your meeting with the filmmaker."

"It went well. He laid everything out for us—what we can expect if we decide to do it…"

"Yeah, I'll just bet."

Savannah turned toward her aunt, a confused look on her face. "What do you mean?"

"There's always more to these things than they reveal."

"Like what?" Savannah asked.

Margaret's dark eyes flashed. "Oh, you never know until it happens. But don't you believe for a second that everything will run smoothly and on schedule, because that won't happen. There will be wrenches in the system—always is."

Savannah squinted in her aunt's direction. "How do you know so much about filmmaking?"

Margaret watched her niece begin to slice the pie before saying, "I've seen movies about filmmaking and I read. I once saw a reality show with these dudes who were making a movie together. You should have seen the problems they ran into." She bounced Lily a little in her arms and said as if speaking to her, "No, doing a movie is not always a slam-dunk activity." She paused, adjusted the baby in her arms, smiled down at her, and then said, "And *your* movie depends on the behavior and mood of a cat—a very opinionated cat, if you ask me."

Savannah turned to face her aunt. "So you think we shouldn't do it?" she asked.

"No, don't let me stand in your way. If you want to do it, be my guest. I just think you should know the reality of moviemaking, that's all."

Savannah frowned while serving the pie. "Maybe it isn't such a good idea, after all."

"Why, just because I pointed out a few negatives? Come on Vannie, it might be fun, and educational, and entertaining. Not to mention lucrative. They *are* going to pay you, aren't they?"

Savannah's eyes lit up. "Yeah—a pretty good sum, actually."

"Then why are you thinking of not doing it?"

Savannah cocked her head and stared over at her aunt. "Uh, well…"

"Oh, you've gotta do it, Vannie. What are your reservations?"

Savannah narrowed her lips. "Well Auntie, you started with the negatives."

"And you're gonna take me seriously? What do I know?" she said with a laugh.

Savannah stared at Margaret and shook her head. She took in a deep breath and said, "Last night I was all gung ho. But this morning, I'm wondering if I want to subject our peaceful household to all that potential chaos. Will it freak out Rags and the other animals? How much of our time will it take? What exactly will be expected of us?"

"Didn't the director…or producer…or whoever…explain all that to you?"

"Yes, but, like you said, there can always be extenuating circumstances. Unforeseen things."

Margaret stared at her niece. "And it's attitudes like yours that keep us from experiencing life and all it has to offer."

Savannah was silent. "Yeah, Auntie, you're right about that. There are many wonderful things in my life that I might have missed out on if I hadn't taken a chance and walked into the unknown. Marrying Michael, having this wonderful child…"

"It's true, Vannie. Everything is unknown until we experience it, right?" She then asked, "How does Michael feel about it?"

"He kind of left it up to me." She thought for a moment and added, "You know, I think I'll tell Rob we'll do it. It will be an adventure and it could be kind of fun. Like Michael and I discussed, it might also be positive publicity for the reading program."

"Good. Can't wait to tell everyone about my cat nephew, the movie star."

"Oh. so that's it," Savannah teased. "You just want bragging rights."

"Ouch, little one, that hurts Great Auntie," Margaret said as she gently untangled strands of her bobbed hair from the baby's grip. She then pulled her phone out of her jeans pocket and handed it to Savannah. "Here, take a picture of me and the princess so I can send it to your mother."

Savannah took the phone. "Okay, smile." She looked at the picture and then at her aunt and said, "Auntie, have you lost weight?"

"A little. Not as much as you have. You look just like you did before you gave birth to this angel."

"Well, thank you. I think I'm just about there. Maybe a few more pounds."

"Then you'll be too skinny. You look good where you are." Margaret studied her niece. "So what size jeans are those?"

"I think they're nines. I used to wear eights. But what about you…how much have you lost? Are you dieting?"

"Just trying to eat better. Max is dealing with a small health issue and needed to change his diet some. I decided to try it myself—makes grocery shopping and cooking easier if we're eating the same things." She stood up, cradled the baby in one arm, and pulled at one side of her jeans. "Yes, I guess they are getting a little loose."

"Well, good for you, if that's what you want," Savannah said.

"What I want is to be thin like you," she said. "But that's not going to happen. You're the only modern-day Brannon to get the tall, fair genes. Even your sister is dark and squatty like your mom and me."

Savannah put her hand over her mouth and gasped. "Yikes, you'd better not let Brianna hear you call her 'squatty.'"

Margaret set Lily in her infant swing and knelt down to her level. "I'll bet you're not going to be short and you certainly didn't get the Italian coloring, you sweet blue-eyed girl," she cooed.

"Yes, the pediatrician says she is high average on the height scale. She predicts Lily will be over five-eight."

Margaret looked up at Savannah, "So she'll outgrow the chubbies?"

"I'm pretty sure, Auntie," Savannah said with a smile. "I've seen pictures of Adam when he was a baby and he was plump, too."

"Now he's a miniature replica of his good-lookin' dad, don't you think?"

"Oh yes," Savannah agreed. She then glanced at her watch and said, "I have a meeting this afternoon with Glenda Cathcart to talk about the reading program. Do you want to stay?"

"When?" Margaret asked.

"In a little over an hour. I need to feed Lily and get her down for a nap."

Margaret thought about it for a moment. "I think I'll pass. I'll get out of your hair so you can get things ready. Sorry for taking up your time this morning." She bent down and tickled Lily's tummy. "I just miss this little girl—need to have my Lily fix. Isn't that right, pretty girl?" she cooed as the baby smiled, gurgled, and kicked her feet.

***

An hour later, the doorbell rang and Savannah rushed to welcome Glenda Cathcart. "Come in."

"Thanks," Glenda said, stepping inside. She looked around. "What a nice home. Always wondered about this place. What's the history?"

"This is the old Forster home, built around 1900. My aunt married into the Forster family and she ended up with the house. When she married Max Sheridan, she moved into his place next door and Michael and I eventually bought this property from her."

"Nice."

"We really love the old place. Michael is a weekend renovation warrior, you know. So he enjoys the opportunities and challenges a place like this can offer. He's done some nice upgrades."

"I didn't realize that. I know your husband, though, as a veterinarian. We've taken our Lab to him a few times."

"Oh, small world."

"Small community," Glenda said with a chuckle.

"Would you like a cup of tea?" Savannah asked. "We can sit in the dining room."

"That would be nice."

Once the tea was poured, Savannah set a plate of fruit-filled cookie bars on the table and the two women sat down. "Apricot and plum filling from our orchard," she said, motioning toward the cookie bars.

"They look scrumptious. So you're into home-canning?"

"Yes. Ever since we brought the old orchard back to life, I feel obligated to use its gifts. So I can fruit and make jams. I also freeze some of the fruit."

"You do all of that with a baby?"

"She's a marvelously good baby, but we haven't had a harvest since she was born. I hope she likes watching me do canning this summer." Savannah laughed. "Maybe she'll want to help someday." She glanced toward the doorway and said, "There's one of my greatest obstacles when it comes to getting things done around here."

"Oh, look at this. Isn't he regal? Is this Rags, the therapy cat?"

"Yes," Savannah said. "But he's also a kleptomaniac, so guard your purse. He's a thieving snoop," she said with a laugh.

Glenda chuckled. "Should we run a background check on him before allowing him on the library grounds?"

Savannah shook her head. "Wouldn't do any good. He's now considered one of the team down at the sheriff's office." She leaned toward Glenda and lowered her voice. "He's their favorite snitch."

"I've read about him. That's hilarious," she said. "Does he have accomplices or is he an only pet?"

"No, we have Walter…he's curled up under the afghan on that dark-plum chair in the living room. He's black and easy to miss. Buffy is part-Himalayan. She's probably in with the baby—loves the baby."

"Gasp! Isn't that dangerous?"

"No, it's not dangerous for a cat to be with a baby, unless a large cat were to lie across a tiny baby, perhaps, or scratch the baby. But Buffy isn't interested in getting in the crib. She doesn't actually pay much attention to Lily. She just likes being in the room with her, especially when she's sleeping. When Lily wakes up, here comes Buffy to let us know naptime's over."

"How cute," Glenda said.

"We also have a dog. She's out in her pen enjoying the sunny day. Do you have children?"

"Yes, a boy, eight and a daughter who's thirteen."

Savannah leaned forward. "Tell me how you came to be a librarian."

Glenda took a bite of a plum-filled cookie bar, then swallowed a sip of tea. She said, "I've been working within the library system for about ten years. I started out as a volunteer. I've always loved books and being around them. I knew, by the time I was in college, that I'd either be a librarian or I'd own a bookstore. I was assistant librarian at another library branch when Leslie got…sick. I was asked to take her place temporarily and it worked into a permanent position." Glenda looked at Savannah. "Did you know Leslie Sparks?"

She shook her head. "My aunt knows her. She said she was librarian for a long time and then she just disappeared. Is she still living?"

"Oh yes, I think so. She had a breakdown of some sort. As far as I know, she's still in a care facility."

"What a shame. How old is she?"

"About my age, actually—maybe thirty-eight or forty."

"I wonder what caused her breakdown," Savannah mused.

Glenda placed the cookie on a napkin and folded her hands in front of her. "Her husband disappeared, you know. Some think he met with foul play. There was something mysterious going on around that whole thing. Leslie was a very pretty woman." She laughed. "Not your typical librarian," she said, pushing her large-framed glasses up on her nose. "In fact, she was stunning. Could have been a model or an actress. I didn't know her well—we attended some of the same functions, and I worked with her a few times before taking over her position. From my vantage point as an employee in the library during that time, I could see that she had some drama going on in her life—you know—personally. When her husband disappeared, things got pretty crazy at the library. Strange people were coming in at odd hours and doing odd things and boy, were the rumors flying."

Savannah frowned. "Strange people doing odd things? Like what?" she asked.

Glenda rested her chin in her palm and spoke more softly. "Renovation."

"Renovation?" Savannah looked confused. "Why would that be odd?"

"Well, I don't think the workers were…you know…sanctioned by the library system, and they were coming in at odd hours—after hours. I don't even think most of the employees and volunteers and—certainly, patrons—knew it was even going on. I came in early and stayed late in those days, trying to take up the slack for poor Leslie. She was terribly overwhelmed."

"Did you ask her about the construction projects?" Savannah asked.

"Sure, of course, but I never got a straight answer. By then, Leslie was pretty well off in that fog." She thought for a moment and added, "She could have been taking some sort of drug. And suddenly she was hospitalized and the rumors really revved up. I haven't thought about all that in a long time."

Savannah sighed deeply. "I guess we just never know what's going to happen to us, do we?" She stood and picked up the teapot off the warmer on the buffet. "Here, let me warm up your tea and we'd better get some business done before the baby wakes up and before you have to head back to the library."

Glenda smiled widely. "Yes, good idea. But I've enjoyed the chatting. I don't get out much with female friends, anymore. My world is kind of one-dimensional." She patted Savannah's hand. "This has been fun."

Savannah smiled. "Yeah, I've enjoyed it, too." She placed the teapot on the warmer, sat down, and asked, "So, how did the school district respond to our idea?"

"They love it!" Glenda said with animation. "They'd like to receive a formal proposal and then we can move forward."

"Is there any chance that we can test the program in the meantime?" Savannah asked.

Glenda hesitated, brushing strands of her thick brown curly hair from her face. "Yes, I think that would be a good idea, actually."

"It would be useful from our point of view—to learn which of our cats will work for this program, how long the various cats can go before they need a break, how to help students relax with the animals so they both stay calm, and so forth."

"I get it. Yes, let me see about pulling together some of our homework students for a couple of reading sessions."

"Homework students?" Savannah asked.

"Yes, they come to the library after school and hang out until their parents get home from work," Glenda explained.

Savannah sat back in her chair. "Sounds good. So when can we start?"

Glenda thought about it and said, "How about Thursday? School's back in session after spring break. I'll get maybe four students to participate and you can use the secret garden."

"Is it secure?" Savannah asked. "I mean, cats can't escape from there, can they?"

"No. It's all enclosed—just open to the sky on top. It's quite charming. You've never seen it?" she asked.

"No, I'm sorry to say. But I'm sure I'll be bringing Lily to enjoy the library in a few years." Savannah looked over at the baby monitor. "Speaking of our cherub, it sounds like naptime's over." She stood and headed toward the nursery. "Yup, here comes Buffy, like clockwork."

"What a beautiful cat," Glenda said when she spotted the small fawn-and-brown cat. "Is she friendly?"

Savannah bent down and ran her hand over Buffy's fur. "Very—she loves attention and a warm lap. I'll be right back," she said as she continued down the hallway.

"Sure."

When Savannah returned with Lily, who was wearing a fresh diaper under her lavender-print bloomers and matching baby dress, she noticed a lot of kitty activity around Glenda. "You've attracted the whole menagerie there," Savannah said with a laugh.

"I guess so. I lifted Buffy to my lap and then Rags and Walter decided to join us."

"Uh-oh," Savannah said. "Rags has found something interesting in your purse."

"Oops, what is that?" Glenda tried to get a look at what he was walking off with. "You know, I think it's just an old receipt. Nothing I need. Let him have it," she said.

At that, Rags stopped, dropped the piece of paper, and headed back toward Glenda's purse. Both women began to laugh.

"Well, for heaven's sake," Savannah said. "I've never seen him do that. He heard you say you didn't want it, so neither does he. He'd rather dig up something you can't live without."

"No, no!" Glenda said, lifting her purse off the floor and quickly zipping it up. Rags wasn't so easily deterred, however. He continued to stand on his hind feet and reach for the purse with his front paws. Glenda frowned as if in disbelief. "This is the cat you want to bring into the reading program?"

Savannah laughed out loud. "Doesn't appear to be very well-behaved and docile, does he?"

"No, he's rabidly going after my purse." She chuckled. "Will the children be safe with this animal in the building?"

Savannah laughed.

Glenda looked down at the cat in her lap. "Will you bring this sweet thing?" she asked.

"We're thinking about it. We're just not sure she'd be comfortable with several children in the room at once." She adjusted Lily's little socks and then said, "Oh, Glenda—I don't think I told you—there's a documentary filming crew coming here to film Rags and we'd like to get some video of the cats and kids in the reading program. What do you think?"

"Documentary? Wow!"

"Yeah, they're interested in filming Rags because of his…um…contributions…to some of the recent criminal cases, and I thought we could work in some publicity for the reading program, as well."

Glenda raised her eyebrows and looked down at Rags, who was now sitting a distance away staring back at her. "That ought to be fun to watch. Sure, we would welcome some positive publicity for the library and for the reading program."

***

Two days later, Savannah left Lily at Margaret's while she and Rags went to their first reading session. Two Alliance members met her there with their cats. Colbi brought Dolly, her eight-month-old tabby kitten, in a small cat tote, and Janice carried her angora cat into the library in her arms. The white angora wore a harness and a leash.

The women had arrived early so the cats could become familiar with the place before being introduced to the students. Glenda pointed the way to the secret garden. Once inside the enclosed courtyard, Savannah opened the door to Rags's carrier. He stepped out and immediately began investigating. Using most of his senses, he examined, sniffed, listened, and felt his way around the courtyard, tasting a few bugs and weeds along the way. Dolly was more fascinated with her old buddy Rags than with her surroundings. She tagged along behind him, batting at his tail every once in a while and playfully attacking his back legs. Janice's angora Bayley, was content just to lie in her lap, casually observing the other two cats.

After several minutes, Glenda peered into the secret room. She noticed Rags sprawled across the seat of the whimsical throne replica batting at one of the many colorful decorations adhered to it.

She grinned. "What's he doing, trying to remove that big daisy?"

"Who knows?" Savannah said.

The librarian glanced across the courtyard and noticed that Bayley was still comfy on Janice's lap. "Where's the other cat?" she asked.

"Playing hide-and-seek," Colbi said, motioning toward a large potted plant with drooping leaves. Just then, Glenda spotted the young tabby pawing at a leaf, a cobweb draped over her ears.

"Looks like she's been where no duster has been before," Glenda said with a chuckle. She asked Savannah, "Okay if I bring in the children?"

Savannah looked at the other two women, who both nodded. "I think we're ready," she said.

Glenda opened the door wide and walked through it. Three students strolled in behind her—all of them full of curiosity as they glanced around the room. Glenda put her hand on the boy's shoulder. "Ladies, this is Jerome," she said. "He's nine." She turned to one of the girls. "This young lady is Gloria, and," she nodded toward the third child, "this is Jasmine. They're both eight."

The three women acknowledged the children with wide smiles.

"Savannah, I'll let you take it from here," Glenda said, just before slipping out through the door and back into the library.

"Hi kids, I'm Savannah and this is Rags."

"Rags?" Jerome said crinkling up his nose.

"Yes, it's short for Ragsdale."

"Ohhhh," the two girls remarked.

"This is Colbi and her kitten. Dolly's only eight months old."

"My baby sister's eight months old," Gloria said excitedly. Then she frowned. "Sometimes I'd rather have a kitten."

The three women attempted to stifle a laugh.

"The white cat on Janice's lap over there is Bayley. She's a lot older than Dolly."

"How old?" Jerome asked

Janice responded. "In cat years, she's fourteen. But in people years, she's around the age of your great-grandparents."

"Whoa," Jerome said.

"My grandparents died," Gloria commented.

"How old is that?" asked Jasmine shyly.

"Seventy-six or eighty," Janice said.

Savannah took the stage again. "Okay students, what we're going to do today is read to cats."

Gloria made a face. "I don't like to read."

"But our cats would love to hear you read. Won't you please read a story to them?"

The students nodded obediently. Jasmine knelt down and began petting Rags, who had left the chair and sidled up to the girl. He sniffed her face and her hair and she giggled. "He tickles," she said.

Jerome plopped down on the whimsical chair.

"Did you each bring a book with you?" Savannah asked.

"I did," Jerome said.

Jasmine nodded and held up her book.

Savannah pointed. "Gloria, there are some books on that table, if you'd like to choose one."

Once the children each had a book in their hands, Savannah said, "Now we need to be quiet and calm so we don't frighten the cats. I want you to find a comfortable place to read. It might be over there in the corner under that tree, or you can lie on the bench or sit on the floor on these colorful pillows." Look, there's Dolly lying in the sunshine in that big flower pot."

Everyone laughed.

"One of you might like to pull a chair over near her and read your story to her."

"I have a book about a puppy," Jasmine said.

"I'll bet she'd love to hear that story, Jasmine. Why don't you go sit near her and begin reading." Savannah glanced at the other children. "Jerome, I see that you're engaging Rags. Would you like to read your story to him?"

"Yeah, okay," he said without much enthusiasm.

"Gloria, that sweet angora cat Bayley doesn't have a partner. Would you like to have her sit on your lap while you read?"

Her eyes lit up. "Yes!"

Soon the children seemed to feel somewhat comfortable reading out loud to the cats, and they began to relax. The three women walked to the far side of the courtyard and watched inconspicuously.

After a few minutes, Savannah noticed that Jerome was distracted. She walked over to him and asked quietly how things were going.

"He's playing with my shoelaces," he said. "He's not listening."

Savannah observed the situation for a moment. "How about if I sit here with you for a little while and see if I can get Rags to settle down." When the boy agreed, Savannah knelt next to him. "Okay, I'll pet him while you continue reading. Try not to wiggle around too much. When you wiggle, he thinks you're playing. Just sit still and concentrate on reading," she said in a soothing voice.

Jerome read two more pages and then quietly said, "He's sleeping. How's he going to hear my story if he's sleeping?"

"He's not really sleeping. He's just resting. He's relaxed. Watch this," she said as she ruffled the fur gently on his head. Rags lifted his head and opened his eyes. He then laid his chin on his outstretched legs and closed his eyes again. "There, see? He's just resting. I think he wants to hear the rest of your story."

Jerome appeared satisfied with Savannah's explanation and she left him and Rags alone.

A few minutes later, Jasmine raised her hand and Savannah walked over to her. "I finished my book," she said.

"Good. Did Dolly like the story?"

"I think so. She listened to me read." Jasmine petted the kitten and then asked. "Can I read another book to her?"

"Sure can—come on, let's choose one."

Another ten minutes passed, and Savannah asked quietly, "How's everyone doing?"

There were no comments.

"Were the cats good listeners?"

"Yeah," the children said, echoing one another.

"Do you think the cats liked the story you read?"

Gloria's face lit up. "Bayley purred when I got to the good part."

"Then she must have really liked it."

"How did you and Rags do?" she asked Jerome.

"He's the only boy cat, isn't he?"

"Yes, I guess he is."

"And I'm the only guy. Us guys read a guy book."

"Did he like it?" Savannah asked. "Did he listen when you read?"

"I think so," Jerome said. "But sometimes he pawed at the pages like he wanted me to turn them faster." He thought and then said, "Or maybe he was pointing to the pictures."

Savannah smiled at the boy. She then addressed all of the children. "So tell me, would you like to do this again?"

The students shouted, "Yes!"

"Cool. Then we'll be back and you can read to the cats again."

"Can I read to Rags?" Jerome asked.

"And I want Dolly," Jasmine said.

Gloria chimed in. "I love Bayley. I think she's the only one who ever liked hearing me read."

"Well that was a smashing success," Savannah said enthusiastically after the children had left. She, Colbi, and Janice did high-fives all around.

"This was so neat," Janice said. "Thank you for letting me be a part of it."

"Certainly," Savannah said. "We appreciate your sharing Bayley with us. What a sweetheart. And what a difference she seemed to make for little Gloria."

"I just want to take Jasmine home, she's so cute. I think Dolly would, too," Colbi said with a smile. She then lurched forward and pointed. "Savannah, what's your cat doing?"

"Oh my gosh, I forgot all about him." She headed toward him. "Where does he think he's going?" By the time she reached him, he had gone down three cement steps and was standing with his paws on the solid wall at the bottom. "What are you doing, Rags? Looking for a way out? Huh?"

"That's strange," Janice said, joining her. "It's like he wants to see what's on the other side of that wall…like there's something of interest to him behind it."

Savannah smiled. "Like a secret of some kind? Yup, he's good at conjuring up secrets."

Colbi walked over to where the others stood, leading Dolly on her leash. “What lies beyond the wall?” she said, using an eerie tone to her voice.

When all three women had converged upon him, Rags sat down on the bottom step and stared up at them.

Janice laughed. “I don’t think he likes us making fun of him.”

“No he doesn’t, do you Rags?” Savannah said. “But he’s kinda used to it. He gets it a lot.”

“How’d it go?”

The trio turned toward the voice. “Oh Glenda. Great!” Savannah said. Janice and Colbi nodded.

Glenda was beaming. “The kids sure seemed happy. Said they want to read to cats again.” Then her demeanor changed. She looked over at Rags and asked, “What’s he doing?”

“Good question,” Savannah said. “He seems fascinated with the wall or whatever is behind it. Do you know what’s behind it?”

Glenda shook her head slowly. “Well nothing, actually. It’s just a wall. There’s an enclosed deck on the other side of it with another cement wall separating it from the parking lot. Why someone put stairs right there is anyone’s guess.” She paused and added, “You know, there’s some quirky construction designs in many of these old buildings.”

“Maybe the builder was the one who designed the old Winchester house,” Janice said.

Glenda nodded. “Where there are all those staircases and doors that lead nowhere?”

Savannah grinned. “Stairs that go nowhere? Kind of adds to the fairytale atmosphere here in the secret garden, don’t you think?”

***

That evening over dinner, Savannah told Michael about the reading program. "Oh, Michael, it was magical. The children loved it. The cats were perfect. I had such a wonderful time." She placed three spears of asparagus on her plate and added, "I'm beginning to wonder if I should have become a teacher rather than a veterinarian." She tilted her head a little. "Well, I could teach children about animals."

"Or teach animals about children," Michael said, straight-faced.

"What?" she said scrunching up her nose.

"You're so cute when you get all obsessed about something."

"Obsessed?" she snapped.

"Yeah, you know, excited…" He cleared his throat. "How did old Rags do? Was he a good boy?"

"He was. You'd be a proud papa." She took a bite of her salad and then waved her fork in the air, swallowed, and said, "Oh, he found a curiosity."

"A curiosity?"

"Yes. There were these stairs that went nowhere and he wanted to know what was behind door number one."

"Huh?" He frowned. "Door number one? Where were you, on the Price is Right?"

"No. But someone built a wall where there shouldn't be a wall, at the bottom of some cement stairs, like at the old Winchester house in San Jose." She cocked her head and said, "Or they built stairs where there shouldn't be stairs up against a solid wall."

"Now that's interesting," Michael said. "I'll have to go over there and take a look."

"Oh, Michael, I called Rob Willoughby and he wants to start filming right away. He'll have a crew here Monday."

"Whew, that soon, huh?" Michael said. "What do we need to do in preparation?"

"I don't think anything, really. I'll have to arrange for another reading group at the library. I think Rob's people will get in touch with Craig, Damon, and Colbi—probably Auntie."

"Why?" he asked.

"Well, they'll be interviewed for the film. They've all been involved with some of Rags's quirky behavior. They'll be part of the documentary."

"Oh, so it's not just a cute cats segment," Michael said. "People will speak, too?"

"Yeah, since cats can't speak," Savannah said, laughing. "Do you think Charlotte would like to be a part of it? She discovered some of the clues, which helped solve Craig's criminal cases, in Rags's stash."

"That's a good idea. Let's check with Reba first. She may want to learn more about Rob's intentions before letting her daughter get involved. So where will the film crew stay?"

"They'll get several rooms at the Capri."

"Several rooms? How many people are coming?"

"I guess some of them travel with their spouses," Savannah said. "Rob asked about an RV park. Some are evidently coming in their motor homes."

"Caravan style? Like "Westward Ho" or something?" Michael asked. "Could get interesting, I guess."

Chapter 3

"So are we set to film at the library?" Rob asked when he called Savannah Tuesday afternoon.

"Yes, at three thirty tomorrow. Now, it's a rather small space and we don't want to freak out the cats or the children; can we keep the number of cameras and people to a minimum?" she asked. "We've only done the program twice and it went well, but you'll be adding a dimension we haven't encountered."

"Yeah," Rob said, "I have an experienced animal videographer. We've worked together before. In fact, he's from this neck of the woods. Maybe you know him. His name's Lance Grayson."

"No," Savannah said. "The name's not familiar. My aunt may know him; she's lived here all her life. Was he doing filming when he was here before?"

"I don't think so. I believe he was in construction."

"Okay, is there anything we need to do to prepare?" Savannah asked.

"Not a thing," he said. "Just be there with the cats and the kids. Set the stage for us."

***

Wednesday afternoon, Savannah and Michael pulled into the library parking lot.

"Thank you for taking off early this afternoon, hon," Savannah said.

"Not a problem. We didn't have much going on today. Anyway, Lily and I want to see all the activity, don't we, baby girl?" he cooed as he removed her from the infant car seat and tucked her into a baby carry pack he had strapped on.

Suddenly, they heard, "Hi you two."

Savannah and Michael looked up. "Oh, hi, Damon," Michael said. "On assignment?"

"Yeah. And I thought it would be fun to watch little Dolly and Mr. Rags in action."

Savannah chuckled. "Actually, there's not much action—at least we hope there won't be. The cats are just supposed to sit quietly and listen."

"That, I gotta see," Damon said, shaking his head. "Usually Dolly is just racing all around Colbi's place—up and down the stairs, over the furniture. Colbi caught her on top of the fridge the other day."

"On top of it? How...?" Michael started.

"We figure she jumped up on the stove and then made the leap to the refrigerator," Damon said. "Can't have her up on that stove. Could be dangerous. Oh, and she gets inside the refrigerator."

"Inside?" Savannah said. "Cats don't usually like cold places."

"Yeah, but she knows there's food in there. She does like to eat, ever since you got her well, Michael." Just then, Damon made eye contact with Lily. "Hi there, pretty girl," he said as he reached out to touch her cheek.

Everyone laughed when she kicked her feet and waved her hands in excitement.

"I think she likes you, Damon," Savannah said.

He smiled down at the baby. "Well, I like you, too, Lily." He stood straight and said to Savannah and Michael, "I don't think I've ever been liked by a baby before. You know what? It's cool."

Savannah and Michael laughed. "Oh, here comes Colbi," Savannah said. The trio watched her pull into the lot and park her car.

Damon walked over, opened the passenger door, and peered in. "Hi Dolly," he said, lifting the carrier.

Colbi leaned toward him and they kissed. "Thanks," she said. "She's getting heavy."

Michael chuckled. "I guess so, if she's climbing in the fridge and helping herself to the food."

After exiting her car, Colbi walked up to Lily and greeted her with a smile and a kiss on the cheek. Lily smiled back and kicked her feet.

"She's happy to be out and about," Damon said.

"She's always happy," Colbi said. "Aren't you, sweet pea?"

Savannah opened the side door of their SUV and prepared to lift their cat carrier.

"Here, I'll get the cat, Savannah," Michael offered.

Savannah shook her head. "Oh, I can get him. You just take care of the baby."

"Here, Savannah," Damon said, "you take Dolly and I'll carry the big guy."

"Oh thank you," she said. "I like that idea."

Once they were inside the main part of the library, Glenda greeted Savannah and Colbi, who introduced the librarian to Damon and Michael. They walked out to the secret garden together.

"Just put him anywhere," Savannah suggested, referring to Rags and his carrier.

"Hey, this is cool," Damon said looking around.

Michael agreed. "I didn't even know it was here."

"How many students do we have today, Glenda?" Savannah asked.

"The same group of three. I thought it would be wise to invite the same children who are already comfortable in the program. I just hope they'll be able to relax in front of the film crew."

"From what I understand, they'll be as inconspicuous as possible. The videographer is accustomed to shooting animals." Something caught Savannah's eye and she said, "Oh, here's Rob. Rob this is Glenda Cathcart, the librarian." She motioned toward Colbi. "You met Colbi yesterday, right?"

"Sure did," Rob said, acknowledging her. He nodded in Glenda's direction. "Nice to meet you. Thanks for setting this up. Do we have permission slips from the parents?"

"Yes, right here," she said, handing him a folder.

Savannah turned and saw that Michael and Damon were on the other side of the courtyard and not paying attention, so she said to Rob, "Well, you met my husband. I'll introduce you to the local news reporter in a minute." She smiled at the man walking up behind Rob, noticed that he was laden down with what appeared to be camera equipment, and said, "This must be your videographer."

"Hi, I'm Lance," he said reaching out for Savannah's hand.

"Hello Lance; Savannah," she said, shaking hands with him.

Colbi took his hand briefly in greeting as Savannah looked over at the small book shelf. *Hmm, the children have read most of these,* she thought. Without glancing up, she called out to Glenda.

There was no response. She looked at the librarian and noticed that she was preoccupied, as she stood stock-still, her stare fixed on the cameraman. *That's odd*, Savannah thought. *Does Glenda know him? It seems as though she's trying to place him.* Savannah looked in Lance's direction and noticed that he was busy unloading his equipment, seemingly oblivious to Glenda's presence. *He's good-looking in a schoolboy kind of way,* Savannah observed. *But it isn't a "he's hot" kind of vibe I'm getting from Glenda. There's something else on her mind.* She sidled up to Glenda and quietly asked, "Do you know him?"

Glenda jumped a little. "Uh…oh…I…" she stammered. She looked at Savannah briefly. "I thought I did, actually, but no, I don't think so," she said as she scurried out through the door to the main portion of the library.

In the meantime, Michael and Damon stood on the south side of the courtyard, staring down at the cement steps. "Savannah told me about this oddity," Michael said. "It is strange to see stairs leading slam against a solid wall, isn't it?"

"Yeah, sorta, I guess," Damon said.

Michael studied the situation. "Hey, I'll be right back." When he returned, he said to Damon, "Just as I suspected—this is a free-standing wall. There's a deck on the other side." He scratched his head. "But why the stairs? Very odd construction."

Damon turned and surveyed the open-air room. "Well, the wall almost matches the other three walls. Obviously, in order to secure this space, they had to put a wall here."

"Yeah," Michael said, running his hand through his hair. "I get it. But why these stairs to nowhere? Doesn't make sense to me."

"Michael," Savannah called, "the children will be coming in a few minutes. Do you want to find a place to sit or stand out of the way? We don't want any distractions."

"Can I stand near the door in case Lily fusses?"

"Good idea, depending on where the camera's facing." She addressed Lance. "Which direction will you be shooting?" she asked. "Do you need to take the natural light into consideration?"

"How astute of you," Lance said with a broad smile. "Ever been a videographer?"

Savannah blushed. "No," she said, waiting for his response.

He stared at her, grinning for a moment and then answered, "Okay, how about if I shoot in this direction," he said. "But the lighting here is pretty good at all angles, so the kids and cats can settle wherever they're most comfortable."

Just then the door opened and a plump woman in her fifties ushered Jasmine, Jerome, and Gloria into the room

"Hi Dolly," Jasmine said, rushing over to the kitten's carrier.

Janice scooted in behind her with her white angora in her arms and apologized for being late.

"Hi Bayley," Gloria said, walking up to pet the cat.

"Where's Rags?" Jerome asked.

Savannah scanned the room and said, "Oh, I guess he's still in that carrier over there. Do you want to let him out?"

"Sure," the boy said as he rushed toward the cage.

Savannah called after him, "Remember to move slowly around the cats, Jerome."

"Excuse me."

Savannah turned to face the woman who had accompanied the children. "Oh, hello."

"Hi, I'm a library volunteer. The parents want to know when to pick up their kids."

As Savannah contemplated the question, she noticed that the woman was focused on something across the room. Savannah turned and saw that she was staring at Lance as he worked to set up his camera equipment. *Well for heaven's sake,* she thought. *What's the appeal?* She glanced in Colbi's direction. *She doesn't seem particularly interested in the cameraman.* She took in a ragged breath, shook her head, and said to the volunteer, "In about an hour, I'd say."

"Huh?"

"The parents can pick up the kids in about an hour," Savannah repeated.

"Uh…okay," the volunteer said.

Savannah couldn't help but notice the woman taking one more glimpse at Lance before leaving the courtyard.

***

"That was kinda fun," Michael said as the couple drove home from the library later that afternoon. "Rags gave them some good footage, don't you think?"

"Yeah, I'm pleased. I think Rob was, too. I was surprised the children were so relaxed, under the circumstances."

"It took them a while to get their minds off the camera and begin reading, but once they focused on the cats, they seemed to go off into another world," he said. "It was really interesting to watch." She sat next to him in the car this time because they had such a short distance to go. "He patted her leg and said, "Hon, you're doing a great job with your program. I'm impressed. And Damon is, too. He got a kick out of the cats and the kids. He took a few pictures with his phone, so there may be a nice spread in the newspaper this weekend."

"Great."

"So what's next on the filming agenda?" he asked.

"The crew will be out interviewing more of Rags's friends and associates today and tomorrow."

"Associates?" Michael said with a chuckle.

"Sure, they've already interviewed Detective Craig and Colbi. They want to talk to Deputy Jim… also Auntie, and probably Charlotte. They'll be out at our house Saturday."

"Good, I'll be there," Michael said…at least in the afternoon." He turned toward Savannah. "Did you know there's a storm headed our way?"

"Well, I wondered. It's been kind of cloudy."

"It's supposed to hit Friday and rain all weekend."

"That shouldn't cause any problems, should it?"

"Will they want to film Rags going outside?" he asked.

"I don't know. But I'm sure we can work that out."

The couple rode in silence for a while and then Savannah turned to her husband and said, "By the way, Michael, did you see that woman who came into the secret garden while we were filming?"

"No, I didn't notice. Who was it?"

"That old woman who drives the decorated golf cart around. You've probably seen her."

"Oh yes, I know who you mean. She has flowers and bows and toys all over it."

"That's her," Savannah said. "Well, she came in through the gate and just stood there for a while, watching. She was wearing the most god-awful hot-pink, paisley, polyester pants and a red, big-brimmed hat with huge sunglasses. I don't know how you missed her. I asked if she was looking for someone and she said, 'Not anymore.'" Savannah scrunched up her face. "I got to thinking later that was a strange thing for her to say."

"Well, she's not all there, is she?" he asked.

"I suppose not." Savannah was silent for a few minutes. "I wonder what her story is," she mused, not expecting a response. She thought for a moment and then said, "You know, it appeared to me that she was focusing on the cameraman." She waved her hand in front of her. "Oh, that's ridiculous," she said. "I must be mistaken." She turned toward Michael, "But it sure seemed as though some of the other women were taken by him—so maybe she *was* staring at him."

Michael lowered his brows. "I didn't notice that. Are you sure?"

"Oh yes," she stated with certainty. "I caught Glenda staring at him. She actually became speechless when he arrived. The library volunteer couldn't keep her eyes off him, either. And yes, the more I think about it, I'm certain that the golf-cart lady was gawking at him, too."

"What about Colbi and Janice Tuttle?" he asked, as if humoring her.

"I didn't notice whether he was of interest to Janice, but, no..." she shook her head. "Colbi only has eyes for Damon."

"So you think the women all thought he was good-looking or something?" he asked.

"I don't know for sure. But somehow, I don't believe that's it." She thought about it for a moment and said, "No, it was more of a recognition thing...like they know him or knew him. Michael, I think he has a past."

Amused now, Michael said, "A past? Well, hon, we all have a past."

"Sure, but the way everyone looked at him, I think his could be...maybe sinister."

***

Saturday morning, as predicted, it was raining. A few men from the film crew had arrived at the Iveys' the day before to set up a ten-by-twenty pop-up tent with panels on all four sides. "This is our break tent," the older man, known as Crank, had told Savannah. "We bring in fans for hot weather and a heater for cold weather," he had said. He assured her that they would run the electrical off of a generator that "purred like a kitten." She noticed later that they'd outfitted the temporary shelter with a large ice chest, ashtrays, a trash can, and a table and chairs.

"How many of you will there be?" Savannah had asked Crank and his helper, James.

"Dern near ten," Crank had said. When Savannah looked surprised, he explained, "Well, you got yer lighting people, the editor, clean-up people—we don't wanna leave a mess here for ya—camera guys, Rob's assistant, and some of them bring guests."

"Guests?" Savannah asked.

"Husband, wife…some bring their girlfriends instead of their wives. You know how it is," he said with a wink.

"Uh, I guess I don't," she admitted.

By ten that morning, it was raining pretty hard. Rob had instructed Lance to walk around with Savannah and shoot video of Rags doing what he typically does. He assigned his assistant producer/editor Cheryl, to accompany Lance and take notes. Introductions were informal. *She doesn't leave much to the imagination,* Savannah thought, unable to ignore the fact that Cheryl was wearing skin-tight jeans and a low-cut, breast-hugging mint-green top, covered only partially by a cropped denim jacket that looked two sizes too small.

That's more cleavage than I've seen since I left Los Angeles, Savannah thought. "Pretty scarf," she said, referring to the small floral scarf Cheryl had tied around her neck.

"Thanks." Cheryl reached back and lifted her long, blunt-cut dyed-black hair off her neck, then adjusted the scarf. "I like the fifties look—you know, Fonzie, "Happy Days," and all..."

"This is Julie," Lance said, motioning toward a stout but solid woman who, like Cheryl, appeared to be in her thirties. She had bleached-blond hair, too much eye makeup, and a colorful tattoo showing just above her low neckline. "She helps me with the lighting," he explained.

"Nice to meet you," Julie said. "Great house!"

Savannah reached out and shook her hand. "Thanks."

After a few hours of filming, Rob joined the group in the service porch, where Savannah was trying to lure Rags into a cupboard for a reenactment scene. Rags wasn't in the mood, but he did jump up on the kitty shelf Michael had installed for the cats so they could look out the large kitchen window. Lance got footage of that. He also filmed Rags interacting with Lexie, which was a rare occurrence.

"Are they friends?" Cheryl asked.

Both Savannah and Cheryl were outfitted with portable microphones, and Savannah responded by saying, "Not really, at least in Rags's mind. He allows the other animals to live here, but he knows he's kingpin. Lexie, on the other hand, considers the cats hers. She and Walter were best friends when Rags and Buffy moved in. Lexie doesn't understand why the other two cats won't play with her like Walter does. She's actually kind of a mother hen. She likes knowing where the cats are and what they're up to."

Cheryl laughed. "So you have the kingpin and the mother hen. How would you describe Walter's and Buffy's roles within the household?"

"Well," Savannah said, "Buffy is pretty much the little princess. She's the oldest at around ten years old—so maybe she's the queen bee. She knows her place and demands it, but always in a sweet, non-confrontational way. She's a favorite of any guests who love to have a cat curl up in their lap. As for Walter…" she said, stopping to think about her next sentence. "Walter is kind of a loner. He's dependable. You know just about where he is at any time of the day or night. He still loves Lexie. He's the only one who will allow her to lick him. The other cats don't want any part of Lexie's grooming attempts. I guess you'd say that Walter is an all-around good boy. He's gotta be to put up with the likes of Rags and Lexie."

At that, Rags made a leap down from the kitty perch.

"Does he always jump down like that? Doesn't he use those steps?" Rob asked.

"No, he likes to make the jump. He's pretty athletic."

"He's into extreme sports, huh?" Lance said, laughing.

Rob addressed Lance. "Is it a good time for us to go over the footage you got today?"

"Sure," Lance said, turning off the camera. He packed up his equipment and then reached for his dark-blue flannel shirt he'd left draped over a wooden chair before heading out the side kitchen door.

"Savannah, we'll get back to you in an hour or so and let you know what's next," Rob said. He winked and suggested, "Now go relax."

She nodded, saying, "Thanks."

Once the crew had left, Savannah poured herself a glass of water. She carried it into the nursery, where Margaret had been entertaining Lily. "Hi," she said.

Margaret put a finger up to her lips in a shushing gesture and smiled down at the sleeping baby in her arms. Savannah smiled, as well. She whispered, "Want me to put her to bed?"

Margaret hugged Lily to her, kissed the top of her head, and answered, "If you must."

Suddenly, the two women heard a new voice. "So this is where everyone is."

"Shhhhhh," Margaret and Savannah shushed in unison as Savannah lifted the baby and started to lay her in the crib.

"Wait," Michael whispered loudly. He bent down and kissed Lily, smoothing her soft brown curls before Savannah laid her down.

"So how's it going?" Michael asked, as they walked together down the hallway and into the living room.

Savannah took a few sips from her water glass before responding. "Been a busy morning. Rags got a lot of attention. A whole crew followed him all over the house with their camera, recorder, and fancy lighting."

"Recorder? Was he being interviewed?" He laughed. "What did he say?" He stopped and turned quickly toward Savannah. "He didn't tell any of the family secrets, did he?"

"Pshaw," Margaret scoffed. "Family secrets? What family secrets?"

Rob had just stepped into the kitchen when the trio entered. "We're going to get out of your hair for a while," he told Savannah and Michael. "We're heading downtown for something to eat. When we get back in about two hours, we'd like to shoot some footage upstairs with you, Savannah, Rags, and his…what do you call it… stash?"

"Okay," Savannah said. "I'll fix us some lunch, let Rags have a catnap, and we'll be ready when you return."

"I'd recommend the diner," Michael said as Rob turned to leave.

Rob looked back at Michael. "Oh?"

"They have pretty good food."

"Where is it?"

Lance had just walked into the room behind Rob. "I know where it is."

"Oh, that's right, you used to live here," Savannah said. She turned to Margaret…glanced in Rob's direction. "Rob, you met my aunt this morning. Lance, this is Margaret Sheridan—used to be Forster. Auntie, this is Lance...uh…I'm sorry…"

"That's okay," he said. "It's Grayson." He offered his hand to Margaret. "Nice to…uh… meet you."

Margaret stood as if a statue and stared at the man.

"Auntie," Savannah said, in an attempt to get her attention.

"Oh," she said, jumping a little. "Hi," she greeted, reaching out and shaking his hand. "Are you back to stay?"

Lance studied Margaret's face, frowned, and said, "Not sure. The jury's still out."

Margaret stared at the man for a few more minutes and then abruptly turned and said, "Gotta go guys, if you don't need me anymore."

"Sure, you're excused," Savannah said, "… unless you'd like to have lunch with us. There's leftover lasagna and a green salad with that raspberry vinaigrette you like."

Margaret's face brightened for a moment. Then she glanced at the two men who were leaving through the side kitchen door. "I think I'll take a rain check. I'd better go make sure my man gets his lunch. Thanks anyway." She headed for the front door, opened it, and said, "Holy cow, it's really coming down out here."

"Be careful, Auntie. Do you need an umbrella?"

"No. I'm okay," she said as she disappeared through the opening, closing the door behind her.

"Well that was odd, wasn't it?" Savannah said as she looked from one door to the other.

"What?" Michael asked.

"My aunt's reaction to the cameraman."

Michael thought about it for a moment and then said, "Humph, I guess I didn't notice. What did she do?"

"Well, nothing really. She just…well, I think she knows him."

"Didn't seem like it to me. She wasn't very cordial."

Savannah pointed her finger at Michael. "Bingo, that's just it. She knows him, but she doesn't like him. I think she has some sort of history with him."

"What kind of history?" Michael asked, opening the fridge in search of the lasagna. "Were they involved in a demonstration together—fellow activists?"

"I don't know. All I know is that there was a flutter of recognition, and whatever she recalled about him was not especially pleasant."

As Michael placed the lasagna in the microwave, he said, "Maybe they got arrested together or he left her to take the rap." He faced Savannah, his eyebrows raised. "I know, it was a jewelry heist. She was the ringleader and he ran off with all the loot."

Savannah rolled her eyes. "Michael, be serious."

"I am being serious. What else could it be?"

Savannah took the salad dressing from the refrigerator and shook it before setting it on the table. "It probably has nothing to do with crime, for heaven's sake, unless…" She reached for plates and bowls.

"Unless what?" he asked.

"Well, maybe it was a cruelty to animals or a hoarding situation and she had him arrested." Savannah stopped abruptly and spun around. "Hey, that's my cell. I'll bet it's Auntie with a story about Lance." She smiled as she rushed toward the phone, which was charging on the buffet in the dining room. "Ooooh, I'll bet this is good…"

Savannah returned to the kitchen, cell phone in hand, just as Michael pulled the lasagna out of the microwave. "Was it her?"

"No. It was Iris asking about the shoot today. I told her I'd call her back," she said. "I'll call my aunt later, too. I just hope she wants to talk. I'm really curious now."

***

Two hours later, Savannah carried Lily up the stairs, placed her in a stroller, and wheeled her into Adam's bedroom. Rob and Lance followed. Cheryl was assigned the task of helping the second videographer, DeeDee, film the other household pets.

"So this is the cat's stash!" Rob exclaimed when Savannah opened the closet door.

"Yup. Well, he hides things in other places, too, but this is where we've found most of the incriminating evidence he's discovered over the last few years."

"Like what?" Lance asked, camera lens poised on Savannah.

"A letter that helped identify a dead woman, a business card that turned out to be crucial in Colbi's rescue, a bandana that led to an arrest, a baseball cap…"

"He can carry a baseball cap in his mouth?" Rob asked.

Savannah smiled. "Yes; just look at some of the stuff he's taken recently."

The cameraman zoomed in on the pile of items in the closet. "Is that a wallet?" he asked.

Savannah took a closer look. "Oh my gosh," she said as she picked it up.

Rob chuckled. "Whose is it?" he asked from across the room.

Savannah opened the small canvas wallet and peered at the name on the driver's license. She squinted pensively over at Rob. "It's yours. Robert Z. Willoughby," she read.

Rob quickly stood, patted his back pocket, then dug his hands into the front pockets of his cargo pants. "Well, I'll be," he said. "That little scoundrel must have sneaked it out of my jacket pocket."

Lance laughed out loud. "That's rich. Better count your cash," he said, making sure to keep the camera rolling. "The cat may have stiffed you."

Savannah sighed. "Yes, he actually likes money. We can't leave bills lying around." She began pilfering through the pile of Rags's things as the cat watched. Every once in a while, he'd step in and sniff one of the items.

"Get out of the way, Rags, I want to see if you have any money in here," she said, nudging him back with one hand. After a few moments, she turned toward the others, holding something in her hand. "Well, here's what's left of a dollar bill."

"So he shreds things, too?" Lance asked, laughing again.

"Not always. Savannah said. "Some things he leaves intact and other things he chews to bits. We don't know how he decides what needs shredding."

Rob took a last look at his wallet before stuffing it into his pocket. He shook his head and said, "I don't know how he got his paws on this."

"Savannah," Lance said, still laughing, "you should greet all your guests with chains so they can secure their wallets to their belt loops."

"Good idea," she agreed. "We do have a designated shelf for female guests' purses down in the dining room."

"Really?" Rob said, shaking his head in disbelief. "So what else is in his stash?"

Savannah looked over at Lily, who was currently interested in the mobile spinning around above her. She reached into the closet and pulled out a small stuffed bear. "As you can see, he brings some of the baby's toys up here. And, let's see… here's a potholder, a tea bag—he has a thing about tea bags—some of the pieces to Adam's farm set. Here's a horse, a tractor, a couple of chickens…" She turned to Rags. "Adam looked all over for these when he was here last time."

"What's that paper there?" Lance asked.

Savannah reached for it. She examined it for a moment. "Oh dear!" she exclaimed. "Michael's jury summons. I'll bet he forgot all about this."

Lance had to turn the camera off because he was laughing so hard. "That cat's a riot."

Just then Rags walked into the closet. As the trio watched, he stepped out, dragging something between his front legs.

"What the…" Rob started. "Hey is that a…"

Suddenly Savannah screeched. "Oh no!" She jumped up and took off after the cat, who was heading toward the open door.

Lance, not wanting to miss an action shot, contained his laughter enough to begin filming again.

"Turn that thing off!" Savannah shouted as she continued her pursuit.

Lance raced after her and the cat, camera rolling.

As Savannah entered the wide hallway, she saw Rags begin his descent down the staircase. At the same time, she spotted Michael on his way up. Lance was close behind Savannah, camera still running.

"Stop him, Michael!" Savannah shouted. "Stop him!" But she wasn't prepared for what happened next.

Michael lunged for the cat and grabbed him just before he raced between his legs. "Hey, whoa, boy," he said. "What's that you've got?"

"Never mind," Savannah said. "Just get it from him."

Michael gently released the cat's grip on the silky fabric and then held it up so everyone could see the intricate design of Savannah's sexiest bra.

Amidst a rumble of laughter, she rushed toward Michael and grabbed the undergarment from his hands, wadding it into a ball behind her. "Turn that thing off!" she shouted as Lance focused on her angry face.

Just then they heard Lily crying. "The baby," Savannah said, as she turned and rushed back up the stairs and into Adam's room to find their little cherub fussing. As soon as the baby saw her mommy, she kicked her feet and smiled.

"She was just lonely," Michael said as he walked up behind Savannah.

"She wanted to be in on all the fun," Lance said as he zoomed in on Lily's happy face.

"Are we finished up here?" Savannah asked rather impatiently. "'Cause I'm done."

"Sure," Rob said. "Right, Lance?"

Still chuckling, he responded, "I think we have what we want." He smiled at Savannah, "And more," he said with a wink.

Savannah shot him an exasperated look, pointed her finger at him and said, "Don't you dare use that in your documentary." She picked up Lily and headed out the door.

"What's wrong with her?" Michael asked.

"I don't think she likes her dirty laundry aired," Lance said, bursting out laughing again.

Michael ran his hand through his hair. "Well, you aren't going to use that, are you?" he asked.

"Naw," Rob said.

Michael looked from Rob to Lance and said sternly, "And I don't want you to use any footage of the baby, understood?"

"Sure," Rob responded. "I do understand. Not a problem." He turned to his cameraman. "Hey, let's go see what DeeDee got, shall we?"

"Okay. Meet you in the break tent."

Michael followed Rob down the stairs, which spilled out into the living room. He stood at the bottom of the staircase for a moment, looking in all directions. He walked through the dining room into the kitchen and peered in. *She must be in the nursery,* he thought, as he headed toward the downstairs hallway.

"Are you okay, hon?" he asked when he saw Savannah rocking Lily in the old rocker they kept in the nursery.

"Yeah, I guess. That was just embarrassing. My bra? Really?!! Darned cat!" Savannah spat.

Michael knelt next to his wife. "They're not going to use that footage. Don't worry about it."

"Well, I'm not worried, I just don't like people—men—seeing my underwear. It's… embarrassing," she complained. She looked down at Lily, who had her hands clasped in front of her as she looked up at Savannah. Savannah kissed her little fingers.

Michael brushed a curl from the baby's forehead with his hand and kissed her lightly. Lily looked up at him and smiled.

"Where are those…those men now?" Savannah demanded.

"Out in the tent."

"Good. I'll be glad when they're gone."

Michael frowned. "This isn't like you. What's really wrong?"

Savannah thought about it for a minute and said, "I don't actually know. They just made me so mad making fun of me like that and invading my privacy."

"Invading your privacy?"

"Well yeah," she said, looking up at him. "That was my private bra."

Michael started to laugh.

Savannah stared at him for a moment and then she chuckled a little. Soon both of them were engaged in laughter. Lily looked from one to the other and then she began to chew on her hands and fuss.

"Is she hungry?" Michael asked.

"Yes, probably," Savannah said, as she prepared to feed her.

Michael sat on a stool across the room. "What's up with that lighting gal and Cheryl?" he asked.

Savannah tilted her head. "Uh, Julie? I don't know; what happened?"

"Well, when I walked through the living room earlier, DeeDee—that's the camera girl's name, right?"

"Yeah, I think so."

"She was packing up and Julie walked in. Well Cheryl came from the other side of the room and began snapping and snarling at her."

"At DeeDee?"

"No at Julie—the plump one," Michael said. "DeeDee tried to calm her down, but the busty one—Cheryl—huffed and rushed outside. It was tense in there," he said.

"Gosh, I don't know, I've been with Lance and Rob upstairs. I can tell you, being in the limelight is exhausting. Kinda fun, though, when they aren't photographing my undies."

"So you are having fun?"

"Yeah, I think so. And Rags is eating it up. Do you know if they got any good shots of the other animals down here this afternoon?"

"Yeah, DeeDee told me they got some footage of Buffy sleeping. She woke up and yawned. They thought that was cute."

"Speaking of Buffy, here she comes. She does love being with Lily."

"Oh, by the way," Michael said, lowering his head, "I called Marci and we decided it isn't a good idea for Adam to visit this weekend. I know he wanted to see the filming, but the weather is so bad." He looked up. "I don't think any of us should travel unless necessary."

"I'm glad you made the decision, Michael. I was worried about the driving conditions, too." She asked, "Do you know what the forecast is?"

"More rain, hard at times," he said.

"Oh." She frowned. "Rob said something about a barbecue."

"In this weather?"

"He said they usually do a sort of party after a filming and he wondered where we would suggest doing it. We would be invited, along with Craig and Iris, Damon and Colbi…everyone who was interviewed, from what I understand. It's part of the deal." She smiled.

"Gosh, it sounds like a lot of people. How many could we accommodate here?" he asked.

"Oh, here? Um, well, we had what…nearly twenty here at Christmas. There would be about that many for the barbecue, right?" She thought about it for a moment. "Yeah, we could have it here—they have that nice toasty tent out there. Crank and James can bring in more chairs. There's a heater in it, did you know that?"

"So who's doing the cooking?" he asked.

"They're having it catered. I suggested that barbecue place at the strip mall. They do a good job and they're close." Savannah fastened her nursing bra and said, "I'm thirsty. I'll put our sleeping angel to bed and let's go get some iced tea."

The Iveys were seated at the kitchen table when Rob entered through the side kitchen door. "Hi, you two," he said. He looked sheepish as he addressed Savannah. "Are you still mad at us?"

She waved her hand in the air. "No. No harm done." She looked up at Rob. "All I can say is guys sure have a weird sense of humor."

Rob bowed deeply. "Well, I apologize for my part in embarrassing you. Didn't mean to. But that cat of yours…he is a character."

Meow

"Oh, there he is. Hi Rags. Hey," he said, trying to get a better look at the cat, "what's he got there?"

Just then there was a light rap at the door.

"It's Lance," Michael said. "Come on in, Lance."

"Where's your camera?" Rob asked. "The cat's got something."

Lance started to laugh. "I hope it isn't an unmentionable." Savannah shot him a disgusted look and he said, "Sorry." He stifled a chuckle. "I really am."

"Yeah, I can tell," she said, unable to conceal her disapproval.

"It's a little sock…what's it called?" Rob asked, "…a bootie."

"Darn it, Rags," Savannah said, jumping to her feet and heading for the cat.

"Get it, hon?" Michael asked when Savannah reappeared.

"Yeah, he dropped it halfway up the stairs." She fondled it before placing it on the edge of the kitchen table. "Mom made those booties. I don't want him tearing them up."

"Hey, if you ever decide to get rid of that cat, I'll take him," Rob said.

"Well, there are times…" Savannah threatened. "But no, we've been through a lot with him. I think we'll hang in there for the long term." She turned to the two men. "Did we tell you about the time he was kidnapped?"

"Colbi and Damon told us about that. Would love to hear your side of that story," Rob said. "I also want to hear about when you used to let him out and how he'd bring home things from the neighbors."

"Well, sit down. Want some iced tea or coffee?"

"Yeah, coffee, thanks," Rob said.

"Sounds good," Lance said as he pulled out a chair and sat down.

He asked Savannah, "Did he really take things from the neighbors?"

Savannah nodded and smiled. "True story," she said as she moved over to the counter and began pouring the coffee.

"No Rags!" Michael called out, lunging for the lanky cat.

Savannah turned in time to see Rags trotting off with the bootie, again. "Darn it!" she said, rushing after Michael who was tailing the cat.

Just then the door opened again. Julie leaned in and addressed Lance. "Hey, give me your car keys."

"Why?" he asked, leaning back in his chair.

She walked toward him, holding out her hand. "I want to go into town, that's why," she said. "Gimme, gimme."

Lance studied her for a moment and then reached into his pocket, pulled out a set of keys, and slapped them into her waiting hand.

"Thanks," she said as she leaned down and kissed him.

Lance participated in the kiss, but when Julie left, and he noticed Rob staring at him, he raised his hands and said, "Just friends. Just friends."

Rob shook his head. He noticed that the Iveys hadn't returned yet and he said to Lance, "Man, you get around. I thought you and Cheryl…" Rob cocked his head. "Oh I get it, now I see why you recommended Julie for this job. How long have you known her, anyway?"

"A while. Worked with her in Glendale one weekend. We sorta hit it off, if you know what I mean."

"Yeah, I know what you mean," Rob said, shaking his head in disgust. He leaned toward Lance and asked in hushed tones, "But why would you bring her here? You knew Cheryl was working this job, right?"

Lance squirmed in his chair. When he saw Michael and Savannah return, he said to Rob, "Yeah, yeah. So let's talk about the cat, shall we?" He addressed Savannah, "He used to prowl the neighborhood and steal things—he was a cat burglar?"

"Yes," Savannah said, placing the cups of coffee on the table. She sat down. "I lived in a suburb in Los Angeles, and Rags was allowed to go outside. Nearly every night, he'd come home with things he'd found in people's yards—bathing suit tops, flip-flops, toys… I always marveled when he'd bring dog toys home—I had to wonder where the dog was when Rags ran off with his toy."

"Maybe hiding out from the cat burglar," Rob suggested. The producer pulled out a small pad and pen. "What was the oddest thing he ever brought you?" he asked.

Savannah thought for a moment and then said, "Probably jewelry. He came in one night dragging a pearl necklace."

"Someone left a pearl necklace lying around outside?" Rob asked.

"Or did he take it off some unsuspecting neighbor as she enjoyed an evening on her patio?" Lance suggested, laughing.

"Worse," she said. "He broke into her home.

Both men doubled over with laughter. "Really?" Rob said. "How?"

"Well, this was a hot summer night and it seems that this gal left her window open. He climbed right in and took the necklace off her dresser. Luckily, I found the rightful owner. She had screens put on her windows after that incident."

Rob shook his head in disbelief. "A pearl necklace," he said. "Imagine that."

"Imagine this," Michael said, "Savannah tells me that, on weekends, she would load a wagon with everything Rags brought home, and pull it through the neighborhood in search of the owners."

"And Rags would walk along with me," Savannah added.

"No kidding!" Rob exclaimed. "That's rich," he said as he wrote something on his tablet. "Man, I'd like to have a shot of that."

"So you don't let him out anymore?" Lance asked.

"Not unattended," she said. When Rob and Lance looked confused, she added, "There are too many predators here."

"More predators here than in LA?" Rob laughed.

"Good point," Michael said. "But she means of the furred and feathered varieties—coyotes, owls, eagles, and an occasional wolf or mountain lion."

Savannah laughed. "Yup, so now he just frisks guests."

"You got that right," Rob said. "Michael, did you know he took my wallet right out from under my nose and hid it in his stash?"

Michael cringed. "Oh no. I'm sorry."
"It's okay, we got good footage," Rob said. "And nothing was missing."

"Lance?"

Everyone turned to see Cheryl standing in the doorway, pulling her denim jacket tightly around herself. She said, "Wanna go for a ride or something? I'm bored."

"Uh, my car isn't here right now. Maybe later."

Cheryl stepped inside and closed the door. "Where's your car, Lance?" she asked sternly.

"Uh, Julie had to run an errand."

Cheryl's soft demeanor exploded into rage. "That bitch!" she hissed. She glared at Lance as if she wanted to say something else. Then she opened the door and walked out, slamming it shut.

Rob scowled at Lance. "Buddy, I can't even imagine what it's like being you, and I sure don't want to find out." He stood and slapped Lance on the back. "What do ya say we get out of these fine people's way? Maybe see if Cheryl, DeeDee, and her old man—what's his name, Ray?—want to go get a piece of pie or something."

"Well don't go too far. You know, our friend Charlotte will be here in..." Savannah looked at the clock on the microwave, "…half an hour."

Rob flipped a few pages on his pad. "Oh, that's right." He turned to Lance. "Crank has some snacks out in the tent. Come on, let's go see what he has," he said ushering the cameraman toward the door.

"I don't want to go out there and face Cheryl," Lance said in muted tones.

Rob slapped him on the back. "Hey, you made your bed; you're gonna sleep in it, lover boy. So come on."

Chapter 4

"Are you ready to continue?" Rob asked when Savannah greeted him at the kitchen door an hour later.

"Yeah, I guess," she said.

"Where's the star?"

"Upstairs with Charlotte."

"We'd like to get some shots of him maybe taking something out of a purse or a pocket. Do you think he would do that for us?"

"Shouldn't be a problem, especially if treats are involved," she said with a wink. "Charlotte can get him to do just about anything."

"She may be a little shy with everyone around, though," Michael said.

Savannah nodded. "And overwhelmed by the lights and cameras."

"We've had enough experience filming animals and children that we should be able to make her feel comfortable. We'll give it a good try."

"Have you worked with Downs children before?" Savannah asked.

"Oh, she has Down syndrome?" Rob asked. "Yeah, I have, actually. Severe or mild?"

"I'd say quite mild. She's a delightful child," Savannah said.

"Shouldn't be a problem. I'm sure Rags will help her relax." Rob peered into the dining room and through to the living room. "It's getting pretty dark. We're probably going to need more lighting for shooting this segment, right Lance?"

"Exactamundo," Lance said. He walked into the dining room and glanced around into the living room. "Can we film in this area?" he asked. "There's more space to set up the lights and reflectors."

“I like it,” Rob said. He made a call with his cell. “Crank, is Julie back?” He hesitated and then said, “Would you send all three gals in, please? Have them bring their equipment. Thanks.”

Once the team was assembled, Rob gave instructions: “Lance and DeeDee, I want you both to run your cameras. Julie, arrange the lighting to shoot in this direction—toward the staircase. I think I’ll have the child and the cat sitting on the stairs, if we can get him to stay put. DeeDee, if he wanders, would you pick up the slack with your camera?”

“Sure,” she said.

“Cheryl and I will wear mics. I’ll interview. Cheryl, come in whenever you feel I’ve missed something or we need to change direction.” He looked around at the film crew. “Got it?”

Everyone nodded.

“Michael and Savannah, go ahead and have a seat there in the living room where the child… Charlotte, right?” he asked. Savannah nodded and he continued, “…where she can see you.”

“Where do you want the purse?” she asked.

“Oh, yes, the purse.” He glanced around the room. “How about just setting it there on the coffee table. Would one of you go get…Charlotte, now? Oh, here she comes. Hi, Charlotte. Come on down. Is Rags with you?”

Charlotte stopped at the top of the stairs and stared down at the film crew.

Savannah could see that the girl was a little taken aback, so she walked to the bottom of the staircase and asked, “Would you like to bring Rags down to have his picture taken?”

“Uh…oh, here he comth,” she said, motioning toward the cat, who rubbed up against her leg and then darted down the stairs.

"Come sit on the steps with Rags," Savannah said. "This is Rob and he has some questions for you."

"About what?" she asked shyly.

Savannah smiled. "About Rags."

"Okay," she said, moving slowly down the stairs.

"You want to sit right here for me?" Rob asked.

"Okay," she said, lowering herself down to the third step from the bottom. "Do you want Ragth in the picther?" She asked. "I can go get his harneth and leath."

Michael stood. "I'll get it."

Once Charlotte and Rags were settled and the camera was rolling, Rob began asking questions. "So what's the most unusual thing you have found in Rags's…stash?" he asked.

Charlotte thought about the question. She stroked the cat's fur as he lay at her feet. When she finally spoke, she did so with a sense of great accomplishment. "A thigar," she said.

"A…what…oh, a cigar?" Rob asked.

"Yeth," she said with a big grin.

Michael and Savannah stared at one another. She shook her head and frowned.

"Where do you think he found that?" Rob asked.

Charlotte shrugged. "It wathn't thmoked."

Rob looked over at Savannah and Michael. "Do you know where he would get a cigar?"

Savannah shook her head. "Someone's pocket, I guess," she said.

"Now that's pretty unusual, for sure," Rob said smiling at the girl. "A cat with a cigar… Did he chew on it?"

"Oh no. Ragth ith thmarter than that!" she said indignantly. She smiled up at Rob, holding out one hand. "I made a ring with the band."

Suddenly Lance said, "Well, I'll be." He turned off his camera and twisted to look behind him.

"What?" Rob asked, frowning.

"Where's my jacket?" Lance demanded. "Oh, there it is." He walked over to where he'd tossed his light-blue windbreaker on a dining room chair, reached one hand into the pocket, and pulled out a cigar. "That thief," he said. "He took one of my cigars!"

"You've been initiated," Rob said, laughing out loud.

Lance frowned. "Hey, those babies aren't cheap, you know."

Still chuckling, Rob said, "Yeah, not so funny when he takes something of yours, huh Lance, my boy? Come on, let's finish up here and then you can negotiate to get your stogie back."

Once the camera was rolling again, Rob said, "Charlotte, I hear you've helped Rags solve some crime cases."

Her eyes widened and she nodded, her soft red curls bobbing alongside her face. "Yeth! I found a thcarf, and a note, and a hanky…Detective Craig wanted that thtuff."

"And you won a medal, didn't you, for helping the sheriff's department?" Rob asked.

Charlotte blushed, reached inside her blouse, and pulled out a cat-shaped medal hanging from a ribbon tied around her neck. "Thith one," she said. "I told about thomething I thaw and heard and it helped everyone find the lotht cath."

"You are a remarkable young woman, Charlotte. You know that?" Rob asked.

Charlotte lowered her head and petted Rags.

"Hey, do you see that purse over there on the table?"

"Yeth."

"How about taking the cat over there and showing it to him. Let's see what he does when he sees it," Rob suggested.

Charlotte stood, took Rags's leash, and led him into the living room. She showed him the purse and he immediately jumped up on the coffee table and began sniffing it. Within a few seconds, he had one paw in the purse, then his nose went in. He dug around in the purse, then pulled back, sat down, and looked around the room at everyone. Charlotte turned toward Rob and said, "There'th nothing in there he wanth."

Rob grinned and shook his head. "A discriminating cat, huh? Well, that's okay. So Charlotte, do you have anything you'd like to tell us about Rags while we're here?" he asked.

The girl looked up, glanced at Rob, and said, "Ragth ith my friend."

Rob stared at the girl for a moment and then said, "That's a wrap." He glanced around the room at the others. "Good job, everyone." He then addressed Charlotte: "Honey, you were fabulous. Thank you."

"Can I thee the movie?" Charlotte asked.

"Yes, I'll send you all a copy once it's finished."

"Tomorrow?" she asked.

Rob laughed. "No, probably not for a few weeks." He turned to his crew and said, "Let's get out of these people's hair, shall we? Oh, and barbecue here tomorrow at noon. Then we'll head for home."

There were a few cheers.

Rob glanced out the living room window. "Looks like the rain's letting up. Let's pack up." He then addressed Savannah. "By the way, will you make sure that all of the principals in the shoot are invited tomorrow? We want to thank them properly. That would be the detective, your aunt, that kidnapped girl…what's her name…Colbi, the librarian, and their spouses."

***

The following morning, Savannah and Michael were having breakfast. Lily lay nearby in her cradle swing, batting at a toy that hung above her. Savannah was spreading apricot jam on a slice of toast when she heard her cell phone ring. She stood and headed for the buffet where it was plugged into the charger.

"Hello?" she said.

"Hi, Rob here."

"Hi Rob. What's up?"

"Problem."

"What?" she asked.

"Well, we may be stuck here for another day—we've heard that there was a slide on the road home and we've already checked out of our rooms. Not sure if we should try the alternate route in this rain or…"

"It sure came down all night, didn't it? No, I don't think you want to travel in this. Michael had the news on earlier and they said it isn't expected to let up until tomorrow morning. I'd say, you'd better stay put."

"Just a minute, Savannah," Rob said. She then heard him ask someone else, "What?" When he came back on the phone he explained, "We're out at the RV park where Crank has his travel trailer. They just issued an evacuation order here." His voice became accelerated. "Gads, the river's rising. I can see it lapping at the banks. It's running fast."

"That little creek west of town?" she asked.

"Not so little now. Can't you hear it?"

"Yeah, I hear something. That's the creek?"

"Sure is. I'll get some pictures and show you later. In the meantime, we need to find a place to go. Shouldn't be any trouble getting to your place from town, do you think?"

"No. You'll be fine. But wait, Rob. Why don't you all plan to stay here overnight until the rain lets up and the roads are safe. They can park the RV here and we have plenty of beds. If we need to, we can put blow-up beds or cots in your nice warm tent outside."

Savannah looked up and saw her husband staring sternly at her. She turned away.

"Are you sure it's okay?" Rob asked. "Gosh, that would be great. We should be able to take off in the morning. You are a lifesaver, Savannah. Thank you so much."

"You're welcome, Rob. Just have everyone come over and we'll get situated before the party starts. See you in a bit."

After ending the call, Savannah turned slowly toward her husband with a sheepish look on her face. "I'm sorry, Michael. I really couldn't leave them in such a pickle. They've checked out of their motel already and they've been evacuated from the RV park. The river's rising and they fear it will flood the whole area."

"So you invited them to spend the night here?" Michael said, grimacing a little and shaking his head.

"Yes, I did. Was it an awful thing to do?"

Michael was quiet for a moment and then he said, "No, honey. I would have done the same thing, only…"

"I know, Michael," Savannah said, "we barely know these people."

"Right. But what are you gonna do?" he said with a shrug. "They have no place else to go—we certainly wouldn't want to send them out on the highway in this stuff. Even Lexie doesn't want to go out to do her job in it, do you Lexie, huh?" He smiled down at Lily and then asked Savannah, "Okay, what do we need to do to get ready for the onslaught?"

"Well, Helena was here helping me clean before the filming. So not too much—change Adam's bed, move Lily into our bedroom…"

"Most definitely. We want her right with us all the time with strangers in the house," Michael agreed.

Savannah looked at her handsome husband and asked, "Are we paranoid or what?"

"No," he said in all seriousness. He looked down at their baby and said, "We're being appropriately cautious, good parents."

Savannah grabbed a pencil and paper and began figuring. "We can put Rob and Lance in the blue room, DeeDee and…what's her husband's name?"

"Ray?"

"Yeah, Raymond. They can go in the healing room. Crank has a trailer. He and James can stay there."

"Who's James?" Michael asked.

"He hangs out with Crank. They are the clean-up crew; they make sure the ice chest is full… things like that."

"Go-fers."

"What?" Savannah asked.

"Go-fers," Michael repeated. "They go fer things."

"Yeah, I guess," she said. She then looked down at her list. "Julie and Cheryl can have Adam's room—we'll set up a cot in there."

"Not sure that'll work," Michael said, shaking his head.

She crinkled her brow. "Why not?"

"Remember, I told you they don't like each other."

"Oh, that's right. Let's see, how can we split them up?"

"One of them can sleep on the sofa or we can put a cot in Lily's room. We do have that extra room downstairs that we haven't done anything with yet."

"We'd be opening a can of worms if we have to get that room ready. Let's just make sure we have everything we need out of the nursery, and one of them can sleep in there. Lily can sleep in her portable crib tonight. It's just for one night, after all."

By the time the crew had arrived, the plans were set. Michael and Savannah showed everyone where they would sleep and all six of the inside guests followed along on the entire tour. When they entered Adam's room—the last stop upstairs—Savannah addressed Cheryl and Julie. "You ladies have a choice. You can both bunk here in Adam's room or one of you can use a cot in the nursery downstairs. The baby will be with us in our room."

"I'll take the nursery," Cheryl said, brushing her black side bangs away from her heavily made-up eyes. She looked at Savannah, asking, "Is there a bathroom down there?"

"Yes," Savannah said. "You have a private bath. Julie, you'll share the one down the hall with Rob and Lance. DeeDee and Raymond have a connecting bath."

"Sounds good," Julie said, flashing a smile at Lance, who pretended not to notice.

Savannah didn't notice. "Well, you all get settled; the other guests will be here for the party pretty soon. Will the food be delivered or do we have to go get it?" she asked Rob, who was standing near the doorway of Adam's room with some of the others.

"They'll bring it around two," he said. He suddenly turned toward the window. "Boy, it's really coming down."

"Sounds like hail," Michael said.

DeeDee shivered a little. "I believe it is. Gosh, I haven't seen a storm like this in years." She snuggled against her husband. "Kind of exciting."

"It's kind of eerie, if you ask me," Cheryl said.

"Eerie?" Savannah asked.

"Yeah, here we are in this old house, it's raining cats and dogs…" she glanced down at Rags, who was tagging along with the group, and said, "Oops, poor choice of phrases. Sorry Rags. But it reminds me of an old-timey murder movie. When it gets dark, it'll even be more creepy."

Raymond leaned toward Cheryl and let out an eerie laugh, which made her jump and clutch Lance's arm. He pulled her to him and wrapped both arms around her saying, "Don't worry, damsel in distress, I'll protect you." The two of them laughed heartily.

Savannah couldn't help but notice Julie's expression. *She sure hates that woman,* she thought. She looked at Lance. *Looks like they're being played by the same man.*

"Okay, everyone out of my room," Julie shouted. "I want to change into my party clothes." She put her hands on her hips and batted her eyes.

"Or stay, if you want and watch me." She shrugged, glanced at Lance, and said, "It's up to you."

Cheryl was first to rush out through the bedroom door. "I'm outta here." Everyone else followed behind her, each walking to their respective quarters to freshen up and deal with their belongings.

"Fresh towels and washcloths in the linen closet outside the bathroom at the end of the hall," Savannah announced. "Come on, Ragsy," she urged, "I think someone just drove up—got company…" she sang out.

As Savannah took the last few steps toward the front door, Rags darted ahead of her. He stood with his paws on the windowsill, peering through the stained glass. Just then, the door opened and Margaret and Max walked in. Damon and Colbi followed—all of them beginning to remove their raincoats.

"I hear you have a houseful of guests for the night," Margaret said.

"How do you know that?"

"I called a while ago to see if you needed anything and Michael told me."

"Yeah, some of the main roads are closed," Damon said. "In fact, I may have to go out on assignment at any moment."

"The roads are really getting flooded," Iris said as she and Craig came through the still- open front door.

Savannah reached for Margaret's and Colbi's coats. "Let's hang these in the service porch," she said.

"Here, I'll help you," Max offered.

"Thanks. Can you get Iris's and Craig's coats?" She motioned with her head, saying, "Come on in, everyone."

The group joined Michael in the kitchen just as he was hanging up the house phone. "That was Reba," he said. "She and Charlotte aren't going to try making the drive." He chuckled. "She said the rain freaks her out."

Margaret laughed. "Well, she's living in the wrong part of the world—we get a lot of rain here."

"Not like this," Iris said. "This is one of those hundred-year storms."

"Is Glenda Cathcart coming?" Colbi asked.

"Yeah," Savannah said. "She thought she'd be okay if she sticks to the highway. According to the news, it's the surface streets and bridges where the problems might occur."

"Is she driving by herself? Doesn't she have a husband?" Margaret asked.

"She said he's staying home with the kids. Or he might drive her over and make sure she gets here," Savannah said.

She hung some of the coats on pegs in the service porch and showed Max where to hang the others. Upon re-entering the kitchen, she said, "Glenda sounded reluctant to come, but I kind of guilted her into it."

"How'd you do that?" Colbi asked.

"And why?" Margaret said.

"Well, she's been such a big help with the program and the documentary. I told her we really needed her to be here so we can thank her properly."

"Does anyone want a drink?" Michael asked.

"Sure," Margaret said. "Whatcha got? Something that goes down warm, I hope?"

"Well, we have beer, wine, lemonade, iced tea. I can even make mimosas if anyone's interested."

"Or hot cider—spiked and unspiked," Savannah added.

"That sounds good," Colbi said. "What do you spike it with?"

"Apple brandy," Savannah said enticingly.

"Sounds yummy."

"Where's the crew?" Damon asked.

"Out in their tent thingy," Savannah said. "They created a covered walkway to it, so we can go out and join them in their domain or visit in here—we have choices." She looked toward the living room. "Oh, someone's here. Probably Glenda."

A few minutes later, Savannah ushered the librarian into the kitchen. "Glenda, you know Colbi and my aunt, Maggie."

"Yes," she said, greeting them.

"You met Michael and Damon the day of the shoot."

"Hi Glenda, what can I get you to drink?" Michael asked.

Colbi sidled over to her and said, "The hot cider with apple brandy is yummy."

"Oh that sounds good. Yes. My husband is picking me up later, so I'll have one of those with no regrets."

Just then, Iris walked over and extended her hand to the newcomer. "Glenda, I'm Iris; we met that day at the library."

Glenda nodded. "Yes, I remember."

"This is Craig," Iris said, motioning in his direction. The tall handsome fellow over there is Maggie's husband, Max."

"Hey, there's more than one tall handsome man in the room," Savannah said.

Margaret laughed. "Well mine's the one with the most cat fur on his clothes."

Hearing that remark, Max turned and looked down at his slacks.

"Just kidding," Margaret said. "That was a joke—well, partially…it is hard to get out of our place without the fur following us."

Glenda nodded to Craig and Max, then asked Savannah, "So how did the filming go?

"Good, I think. They sure got a lot of footage—hours' worth," Savannah responded.

"There's the star right there," Margaret said, pointing to Rags as he entered the room. "Vannie, I thought he'd dress for the occasion."

Savannah smirked. "Well, he's already wearing a grey tuxedo…well, sorta." She raised her voice and said, "Shall we join the others out in the tent?"

"Go outside?" Margaret complained.

"It's heated," Savannah said. "Come on, it'll be an adventure."

"You're just in time," Rob said when he saw the group coming down the temporary plank into the tent. "We were just going to run a highlight video—clips from the filming we did. There are chairs enough for everyone. Come on in and sit down; the show is about to start."

Just then, Savannah put the baby monitor up to her ear. "Uh, someone's awake," she said. "I'll be right back."

"The baby angel gets to watch her first movie," Margaret said.

"It's not her first," Savannah corrected. "She has a few videos she likes."

"Is she in this one?" Colbi asked.

"Oh no," Michael said. He looked over at Rob. "At least not in the final documentary, right, Rob?"

"Yeah, that's right." He took a gulp from his vodka drink and gave Michael a sideways glance. "But I did sneak a few shots of her in for this showing. I think you'll enjoy it," he said with a grin.

Savannah headed for the tent exit. "I'll be right back," she said.

Colbi caught up with her. "Oh, let me."

"Are you sure?" Savannah asked.

"Yes. I'd love to."

"She probably needs changing," Savannah warned.

"Got it covered, mama bear. You just relax."

"Well, she's probably hungry. I made up a bottle. I'll go warm it. Meet you back here in a few."

"Look, how cute," Margaret said when the two women returned with baby Lily, a warm bottle of milk, and her stroller.

"Love those snuggy jammies," Iris said.

The baby took one look at all of the smiling faces in the crowd and buried her face in Colbi's chest.

"Awww, she's shy," DeeDee said. "She's sure a doll."

"Let me feed her," Colbi said, reaching for the bottle.

"Okay," Savannah said, as she and Colbi sat down behind Lance and Julie, whose suggestive behavior with one another bordered on inappropriate. Savannah noticed Cheryl, with a beer in her hand, sitting on one of Rob's knees. But Cheryl wasn't paying much attention to Rob; her eyes were shooting daggers at Lance and Julie.

Gads, even the low-budget film crews have their drama, she thought. And then something else caught her eye. Glenda, who sat quietly next to Margaret, was also staring at the couple. *And not with a sense of curiosity,* she thought. *In fact, it's a stare similar to the one I saw on Auntie's face when she first saw Lance. What is it with him? He must have made quite an impression on people in the community when he lived here. I'll have to ask Glenda about him.*

"Are we ready to roll?" Rob asked, slurring his words just a bit. He turned to motion for Crank to start the video and for James to kill the lights, when Cheryl slipped off his lap and fell to the floor. She held onto Rob's neck, so when she fell, she pulled him over and he landed smack on top of her.

"Oopsie," she said. "That's one way to get what I want, isn't it, Robbie?" she said, wrapping one arm around his neck and kissing him hard.

"Hey, you don't have to use trickery," he said, laughing. He lifted himself up off the floor and then pulled her up by the hand. "Okay, the show's over," he said. He laughed. "At least the sideshow." He and Cheryl continued laughing as they found their respective chairs and sat down.

Savannah watched as James grabbed a wad of paper towels and cleaned up the drinks the couple had spilled on the plastic floor. She whispered to Colbi, "Glad they didn't do that in my house." As she continued taking in the activity around the couple, she noticed Cheryl looking in Lance's direction, a wicked smile on her face.

***

After the showing, the lights came on and Margaret was the first to speak. "That was hilarious. I didn't know it would be a comedy."

Rob cleared his throat. "Well, it looks like a comedy of errors. But this is just something we put together for your entertainment today—highlights of some of the more humorous moments."

"I'm curious," Iris said, flashing her eyes in Savannah's direction. "What did you find in Rags's closet that got Savannah in such a turmoil?"

"Just you never mind," Savannah said.

Lance winked at Savannah, who was now holding Lily. "We're sworn to secrecy," he said.

"I didn't know that Rags had done all of that work for you, Craig," Colbi said. She waved her hand in front of her face. "I have to say the bit about my abduction brought back some painful memories."

Damon put his arm around her. "Yeah, some awful memories, but some great results," he said.

Colbi smiled through tears. "Yup, it's all been good since then, that's for sure."

"Max, you were quite dapper in the segment where you cxplained how you figured out where Margaret and Savannah were being held when that creep took them," Iris said. "I loved that shot of you with Layla in your lap."

"Yeah, she's my sit-down buddy," he explained.

"Sit-down buddy?" Iris questioned.

"I sit down and she's in my lap."

"So it wasn't staged for the photo shoot?"

Max chuckled. "Oh, no. That was reality TV."

"What kind of cat is she?" DeeDee asked.

"Her background is probably Persian," Max said.

"I love tangerine fur," DeeDee said.

Colbi chuckled and said enticingly, "Hers is like tangerine-vanilla-swirl ice cream."

Savannah laughed, then turned to Craig. "You're an old hand at being interviewed, aren't you?"

"Yes, unfortunately. It comes with the job. But this was more fun. This time, I knew the outcome of the crimes. Most times, the reporters want answers I don't have yet."

"The appetizers are ready," Rob announced. "Everyone help yourselves. We'll serve dinner in about an hour." He motioned to Crank. "Let's set up the tables."

As just about everyone stood and headed for the serving tables, Damon caught up with Michael. "Hey, I want to talk to you about something."

"Sure," Michael said. "What is it?"

"I want to do some work at Colbi's old house. You know, carpenter work."

"Oh?" Michael said. "What kind of project do you have in mind?"

"She wants to turn a spare room into an office. I thought I might be able to put in some shelves for her," he said. "But as you've observed, I know absolutely nothing about building and construction, except for the few things I've learned by watching you."

"Yeah, you've helped me with a few things. You're a fast learner—I'd say you're a natural."

Damon grinned his sideways grin. "I think you have more confidence in me than I have in myself, there, Michael. But I have been watching some of those home-renovation shows."

"I like 'em, too. They have some good tips for builders," Michael agreed.

Damon ran his fingers through his thick, dark-red curly hair and said, "But I still can't figure out why they put that wall at the bottom of the stairs at the library, or why they put the stairs against the wall, can you?"

"What wall?" Margaret asked as she and Max walked up to the two men, each carrying a small plate of finger food.

Michael took a sip from his mug and swallowed. "You know that patio area at the library for the kids?"

"The secret garden?" Margaret said. "Yes, I do."

"Well, there are these stairs that lead nowhere. Three steps and then a wall."

Margaret tilted her head and furrowed her brow. "That's strange. I haven't been there in years, but I don't remember that. Where, exactly?"

"Let's see; right of the door into the courtyard—so the south side."

"They're the only steps out there," Damon explained.

"Well, when I went there as a kid, there were steps that led down into a dark room where they kept puzzles and gamcs." Margaret smiled. "I used to love being chosen to go down there and get something. It was kind of eerie, strange, and intriguing. I felt as if I was on an adventure."

Michael looked puzzled. "So there was a room there?" He shook his head. "It's gone now." He put one finger across his lips in contemplation before asking, "Maggie, how many steps were there?"

Damon and Michael both waited expectantly for her answer.

Margaret took a deep breath and let it out through pursed lips. "Well, let's see…" she said thoughtfully. "One, two, three…maybe ten!" she exclaimed. "That room was pretty deep into the ground, which is why it was so dark, I imagine."

Damon nodded. "Well, now that makes sense, doesn't it, Michael? The room is below ground level. There are more steps, but they're underground, right?"

"Yeah. But, how odd. Why would they close off that room?"

"Maybe they quit using it," Margaret suggested. "They figured it was a hazard for the children."

"Yeah, a kid could fall down a bunch of stairs like that," Max offered.

"When's the last time you remember that room being open, Maggie?" Damon asked.

Michael chuckled. "Are you interested from a builder's standpoint or a reporter's?" he asked.

"Uh, oh, both, I guess," Damon said with a laugh. "Just curious. It is a curiosity, don't you think?" he asked, glancing back and forth among the three of them.

"A curiosity?" Lance said as he and James joined the trio. "What's so curious? I love mysteries."

Margaret stared across at Lance as Michael responded. "We were discussing that crazy construction job down at the library—where the stairs lead smack into a wall. Ever see a puzzle like that in your travels?"

"Uh, no…don't think I have…" Lance stammered.

"Didn't you notice it when you were there?" he asked.

"Can't say that I did. Why is it of interest to you?" he asked, his eyes piercing into Michael's.

"Well, it's just odd, that's all," Michael said. He turned toward Damon. "I'd like to find out what's going on there, wouldn't you?"

Damon stared at Michael. "You mean tear into the wall?"

"Why not?"

"You'd go to that trouble out of curiosity?" Lance asked, looking at them now as if they'd lost their minds.

"Sure, that's what weekend renovators do," Max said with a laugh.

Lance was not laughing. He appeared to have more to say, when he suddenly looked past the others and said, “Oh, here’s the food. Come on in, gentlemen.”

“I’m going to get another mug of the hot cider,” Max said. “Want some?” he asked Margaret. When she didn’t respond, he looked down at her and noticed she seemed preoccupied. He followed her gaze, which had followed Lance. He creased his brow. “Do you know him?” he asked.

Margaret jumped a little. “Huh?”

“You were staring at that guy…Lance. Do you know him?”

She grimaced. “Um…yeah, actually.”

He lowered his voice. “You don’t seem as though you like him much.”

Margaret took in a deep breath and said, “No, can’t say as I do.”

At the same time, Savannah walked over to Glenda, who was sitting alone at the moment. “The food looks great, let’s go fill up some plates, shall we?”

Glenda stood and grabbed Savannah’s arm. “How well do you know that man?” she asked.

Savannah looked in the direction Glenda nodded. “Do you mean Rob…the one wearing the green sweatshirt?”

“No,” she said, “Lance…in the light-blue windbreaker.”

“Oh, gosh,” Savannah said, “not well. Just met him a couple of days ago. Haven’t even had a real conversation with him. Why?” Savannah asked.

“Well, he keeps looking at you.”

“What?” Savannah said. “Why would he do that?”

“He’s no good, Savannah. Watch out for him. He has you in his sights.”

Before Savannah could fully digest Glenda’s warning, Iris walked up with Lily in her arms. “I think little sweetie here wants Mama,” she said.

"Oh, are you still hungry, baby girl?" Savannah cooed, taking the fussing baby from Iris. "She didn't finish her bottle. I'll see if she wants the rest of it." She put her hand lightly on Iris's arm. "Why don't you go with Glenda through the food line. Save some for me; I'll be back shortly."

Before leaving the tent, Savannah walked over to where Michael stood talking to Damon. "Excuse me, you two," she said. "Michael, I'm going to feed Lily. I'll be back in a bit."

"Okay, honey," Michael said. He kissed Lily on the cheek and patted her affectionately.

Savannah's exit did not go unnoticed.

"Hey, where are you going?" Julie called when she saw Lance head for the exit.

"Bathroom," he mouthed.

This didn't go unnoticed, either. At that moment, Glenda turned toward Iris and said, "Excuse me for a moment, will you? I'll be right back."

Iris nodded. "Sure. I'll hold your place in line."

"Dr. Ivey…" Glenda said, finding Michael in deep in conversation with Damon.

"Oh hi, Glenda. It's Michael. How's your Lab doing?" he asked.

"Good," she said, not wanting to waste time on small talk. "Uh, Michael, I think you should go check on Savannah."

"Why?" he asked, his worry lines evident. "Is something wrong?"

"I can't explain right now," she whispered. "Just make sure she's okay, would you?"

Michael looked toward the tent opening and said, "Sure. I'll go check on her right now." He sprinted out of the tent, along the makeshift walkway, up the porch steps, to the side kitchen door. As he approached it, he could see Savannah through the small window. But she wasn't alone.

Chapter 5

"Hi hon," Savannah said upon seeing Michael enter the room. "Lance has just offered to photograph me."

Lance, startled by the intrusion, spun around to face Michael, who quickly moved to Savannah's side. "Is that so?" Michael said.

Savannah faked interest. "Yeah. He's a portrait photographer specializing in boudoir photography and he thinks I would be a great subject."

"Boudoir?" Michael asked, looking confused.

"Sure, you know—bedroom photography, where you wear next-to nothing. He thought you'd really like to have a boudoir picture of me."

Michael shot daggers at Lance. "Is that right?" He walked toward the photographer and growled, "Don't you think you're out of line? If anyone's going to take pictures like that of my wife, it'll be me. Now you go back out and enjoy the party, will you?"

Lance took two steps back. "Hey man, I just thought…"

Michael leaned in Lance's direction. "Well, you thought wrong." He glared at the man until he left through the kitchen door. Michael then turned to Savannah and asked, "You don't want him to take your picture, do you?"

"No, Michael," Savannah said. "You know me better than that. You've seen how much he's been drinking tonight. It's the alcohol talking. I don't think we can take him seriously, do you? How juvenile," she said, shaking her head.

"So you don't think he's…after you?"

She scowled. “For heaven’s sake, no, Michael.”

He stared hard at his wife. “You’re not attracted to him, are you?”

“Absolutely not,” she said. She reached out and grabbed Michael around the neck with one arm while cradling Lily in the other. “Why would I be, when my husband is so…hot?”

“Well, everyone else seems to be—attracted to him, I mean.”

She smiled sweetly at her handsome husband. “Not me!”

“Okay, then.” He glanced toward the door and said, “Let’s go feed our baby.”

“Together?” she asked.

“I’m not letting either of you out of my sight today.”

Half an hour later, Savannah handed the sleeping baby to an eager Colbi, saying, “I can put her in her stroller, Colbi.”

“When I have perfectly good arms to cuddle her?” Colbi said.

“Keep a good eye on her,” Michael said before taking Savannah’s hand and leading her to the food table.

Soon the barbecue feast was all but devoured. James and Crank began picking up the paper plates, and two large trays of cookies were uncovered.

“This is quite a set-up you have here,” Savannah said to Crank. She leaned toward him and said quietly, “I could do without a porta-potty in my yard, though.”

Crank winked. “It’s better than the alternative, don’tcha think? Ya don’t want these people usin’ your facilities all day and night.”

"Well, maybe you're right." She looked across the tent and saw that Colbi still held her sleeping cherub, and she walked over to her. "Do you want me to take her?" she asked.

Colbi smiled brightly, pushing strands of her long brown hair over one shoulder. "Not really. She's such a sweet armful."

"Boy, you've got it bad, don't you, Colbi?" Savannah said.

"What?" Colbi asked in innocence.

"You know what I mean, don't you, Iris?"

"Sure do," she said, a knowing smile on her lips. She looked affectionately at Colbi, "You, my dear, are ready to nest."

"Yes," Savannah said. "You're poised on the brink of nesting."

"But I'm not ready to have a baby. I haven't built my career, yet. Heck, I'm not even engaged."

"Tell your hormones that," Iris offered.

"Well, I sure do love this little bundle," Colbi admitted. "I can get my baby-fix by visiting her until all of my baby ducks are in a row."

"Sounds like a plan," Savannah said. She looked around. "Where's Damon?"

"He got called out." Her demeanor shifted as she said, "He sent a text earlier…said it's bad out there and he's worried about some of our homeless friends. Rumor is that not all of them left their camps when they were ordered to and they may be in danger."

Margaret, who was sitting across the table from the trio, asked Colbi, "How come *you* didn't get called out? You're a reporter just like Damon is."

"Oh, I believe they still think of me as the weaker sex," she said. "I'll tell you, I don't mind. I'd rather be here all cozy with all of you than out in this storm."

"Now I know she's in nesting mode," Iris said. "Something's wrong when our Colbi isn't up for an adventure."

"Ha-ha," Colbi responded good naturedly. "Maybe I'm just getting more cautious in my old age."

"Old!" Margaret and Iris exclaimed in unison.

Margaret looked at Iris, "Do you remember when we were pushing thirty-five? Did you consider yourself old?"

"Hell, I can't remember. That was—what—over twenty years ago?"

"Get out of my face, you fat witch!!"

"Make me, or are those ugly fake boobs of yours in the way?"

All eyes turned toward the commotion and saw Julie and Cheryl facing off. Just as Julie reached for a handful of Cheryl's thick, black hair, Crank grabbed her arms and held them behind her. Rob rushed to stand between the two women. "Hey, that's enough, you alley cats. You want to scuffle, do it on your own turf, don't be bringing it here," Rob said. "Crank, take her out and cool her off, will ya?" Rob grabbed Cheryl's wrist. "You come with me."

Julie yelled, "Are you crazy? It's raining out there!"

"Sure is," Crank said, as he grabbed his raincoat and ushered her outside.

"Now what's the problem?" Rob asked Cheryl.

She avoided eye contact. "I don't know, she's crazy, that's all…and jealous."

"Well, you two stay away from each other, you hear? I don't want any more trouble from either of you." He took hold of Cheryl's arm and squeezed. "Got it?" he said through gritted teeth.

"Yeah," she said, jerking her arm from his grip. "I got it. Just keep her away from me."

"I apologize for that," Rob said as he approached the stunned onlookers.

"What happened?" Margaret asked.

"Heck if I know—chick stuff."

"Are they always like that?" Iris asked.

He took in a breath. "Well, it's actually the first time they've worked together. They both seem to have a burr under their saddles. I don't know what's going on, but I won't have them working on the same job again."

"Looked like a jealous rage to me," Margaret offered. "Must be a male involved."

"Huh? Those two after the same guy?" Rob scoffed. "I can't imagine." He scanned the group with his eyes and added, "You can't take everything you see here seriously. When you work closely together like we do, you become family—brothers and sisters. There are bound to be clashes and disagreements, especially among the more creative people." He chuckled, "And when they're drinking, even more so." He paused before saying, "Sometimes I feel like a parent trying to keep peace in a dysfunctional family."

***

The next morning, Savannah was up first. "Good morning, sunshine," she murmured as she lifted Lily out of her portable crib next to their bed.

"The sun's shining?" Michael asked, yawning and stretching.

Savannah walked over to the window and pushed the drapes to one side. "Well, it's kind of early to tell, but it looks like a clear sky out there—so yeah, maybe it will be sunshiny today."

"Good," Michael said as he crawled out of bed and joined her and Lily at the window. "Look at all that water. Puddles everywhere," he said.

Savannah let the heavy drapes drop back into place. "Yeah, it sure did rain last night. I bet the sound of it on that metal RV kept Crank and James awake."

"They're probably used to it," Michael said as he headed toward the bathroom. "They live in that thing, you know."

"No, I didn't know that." Before he could enter the bathroom, Savannah said, "Are you going to take a shower?"

"Yes, okay with you?"

"Sure. I'll go start the coffee after I change Lily."

"Aren't you going to feed her?"

"She ate a little while ago, so no, not for another few hours."

Once in the kitchen, Savannah placed the baby in her cradle swing and started to make the coffee. Just then, Lexie stepped out of her bed near the side kitchen door and began staring at the doorknob. "You want out, huh? Okay, come on."

Just minutes earlier, Crank and James had stepped outside their travel trailer for a smoke. They'd barely had time to enjoy the rain-washed morning air when Lexie bounded down the porch steps. Savannah stood at the kitchen door keeping watch over the Afghan-mix dog. She waved at the two men, calling out, "Coffee will be ready in a minute."

When Lexie didn't return right away, Savannah walked out onto the wrap-around porch and peered along the south side of the house. "What does Lexie have?" she asked.

That's when Crank slowly lifted his bulky frame from the lawn chair and ambled toward the barking dog. James, a wiry young man well into his twenties, reached Lexie's side first. Crank arrived just seconds later. He stared down through bloodshot eyes under bushy white brows. Running one hand over his full beard, he muttered, "Well, hell."

"Is she dead?" James asked, his voice quivering.

Crank nodded. "Yeah, she's dead, all right."

"What is it?" Savannah called from the porch, not wanting to walk across the wet grass in her slippers.

"Uh…ma'am," Crank said, "you'd better go get your husband, and call your dog, would ya?"

"What's wrong?" Savannah asked, not one to be sent away from a problem.

Crank walked over to where Savannah stood and said more quietly, "There's been an accident, ma'am. Someone's been hurt. We need to call emergency."

Savannah looked at what appeared to be a pile of clothes draped across the rock edging next to the foundation of the house. Her heart began to race. She called Lexie and the two of them stepped into the kitchen. After picking Lily up out of the infant swing, she rushed to the bedroom with the baby in her arms. "Michael! Michael!" she called, as she entered the room. When she saw him coming from the bathroom, shaving cream on his face, she said, "Someone's been hurt." She hugged Lily to her, burying her face in the baby's neck. Barely able to say it, she blurted quietly, "I think someone's dead out there."

"What? Who? Out where?" Michael asked, his usual calm demeanor obviously unraveling.

"I don't know." She placed the baby in the middle of their bed and grabbed the phone. "I have to call 9-1-1."

Fifteen minutes later, Rob entered the kitchen, DeeDee and Raymond on his heels. "What's going on?" he asked. "I heard sirens."

"Look, there are cop cars outside," DeeDee said. "What happened?"

The Iveys glanced at one another from across the table, unsure of what to say. Finally, Michael blew out a long breath, and said, "There's been an accident."

Savannah held Lily close, pressing her lips to the top of her head.

"What sort of accident?" Rob asked as he headed for the kitchen door that led outside. "Is someone hurt?"

"It looks that way," Michael said. "They've asked us to stay inside for now."

Rob, feeling responsible for the crew, walked from window to window, trying to get a look at what was taking place outside. "Crap, one of my people might be hurt. I'm going out there," he announced before darting out the door.

"What happened?" Lance asked as he entered the room wearing jeans and a t-shirt.

"Someone's been hurt," DeeDee said. "We don't know who, yet. I guess it wasn't you or Rob or us." Suddenly, she said, panic in her voice, "Where's Cheryl?"

"Right here," came a voice from behind them. "Who wants to know?" she asked, pulling her hair up in a knot on top of her head. She stretched and yawned, her crop-top inching up and showing her taut, tanned midriff.

"So we're all accounted for except Crank, James, and Julie, right?" DeeDee asked.

Cheryl dropped her hands and looked around, confused. "Why are we counting noses?"

"Someone's been hurt," DeeDee said. "The police are here."

"Oh, I see that," she said, straining to peer out through the large window.

Just then, Rob stepped back into the house, a somber look on his face. "It's Julie," he said, disbelieving.

DeeDee gasped and put her hands to her mouth. "She's out there?"

"Yes. Looks like she may have fallen from the upstairs window and landed on a pile of rocks."

"Pile of rocks?" Savannah questioned.

"Well, a rock border."

"Oh my God," Cheryl said, now looking somewhat weak-kneed.

"Why do you care?" Lance spat. "You hate her guts."

She scowled at him, pulled out a chair, and sat down at the kitchen table.

"Can I get you a cup of coffee, Cheryl?" Savannah offered, quickly standing and moving toward the coffee pot.

"I can get it," she said. "Thanks."

Rap Rap.

"It's Craig," Savannah said. She stood closest to the door, so she reached over and opened it. "Hi Craig." She grimaced and said, "Sorry to bring you out on such a muddy morning."

"Yeah, it is muddy. I left my boots on the porch. Hope you don't mind my stocking feet."

"I prefer them to your muddy feet," she quipped, failing at her attempt to lighten the mood. "So what's going on out there, Craig?" she asked, her demeanor somber.

"I'm afraid we have a body," he said. He hesitated in order to allow the news to sink in before he continued.

Even though she'd expected that the person out there was dead, it was still difficult for Savannah to hear. She moved toward where Michael now stood at the counter and laid her head on his shoulder. He reached over and took Lily from her, put one arm around her, and pulled her close.

In the meantime, Rob collapsed into the nearest chair and held his head in his hands. DeeDee buried her face into her husband's chest. Raymond embraced her and looked straight ahead, staring into space. Lance stood in place against the doorjamb, looking down at his shoes, and Cheryl held her coffee mug in front of her, peering into the black liquid.

Detective Craig Sledge observed the demeanor of each individual before saying, "I want to look around upstairs. Everyone stay down here until I give you the okay to return to your rooms." He opened the kitchen door and called out, "Gonzalez, I'm ready for you. Bring Conklin, would you?"

Once the other two men had entered the kitchen, also in stocking feet, Craig led them up the staircase. He returned fifteen minutes later and announced, "I'd like each of you to come up one at a time and identify your belongings," he said. "Some of it we're going to take as evidence."

When they called for Cheryl, she explained that she didn't sleep upstairs—nothing of hers was up there. Ramon Gonzalez accompanied her to the nursery where he examined her belongings.

DeeDee was the last one to return from upstairs. "Gosh, I've never been through anything like this before," she said, her eyes wide.

"Like the rest of us have?" Cheryl snapped.

"Okay, you're free to pack your things," Craig said upon reentering the kitchen. "Those bags Gonzalez is carrying contain possible evidence. We'll let you know when it's released. If we have anything of yours, you can pick it up then."

"When will that be?" Rob asked, watching Gonzalez and Conklin exit the kitchen with two large bags.

"It could be weeks or months," Craig said. He pulled a pad out of his jacket pocket, flipped through the pages, and said, "Okay, I've taken statements from the men who discovered the body…Mr. Tibbets and Mr. Crankshaw. I'll need to speak privately with each of you. Michael, can I set up somewhere in here?"

Michael thought for a moment and then addressed everyone, "Why don't we get our coffee or juice and take it into the living room? Craig, you can use the kitchen table."

Savannah took a deep breath. "We have sweet rolls, too, and muffins. You all get settled and I'll bring them in."

"I can help," DeeDee offered.

Savannah stared at her for a moment—her mind a million miles away. Finally, she said, "Thank you. Napkins are in the buffet in the dining room…paper plates and silverware, too. I'll get the cream and sugar and we'll bring the coffee pot into the dining room. Oh, and I have a bowl of cut-up fruit." Before leaving the kitchen, she asked Craig, "Can I get you a cup of coffee?"

"I'll get it," he said. He then turned to Rob. "I'd like to talk to you first, if you don't mind."

***

Nearly two hours later, Craig sauntered into the living room where Michael and Savannah rested. Lily slept nearby in her cradle swing.

"So how did it go?" Michael asked, opening his eyes and raising his head off the back of the sofa. Savannah, who had dozed under a throw in the overstuffed chair, sat up and put her feet on the floor.

"No work today?" Craig asked when he saw Michael.

Michael shook his head. "I may go in later."

The detective walked over to the cradle swing and stared down at Lily. "So innocent," he said. "The world needs more innocence." He touched Lily's cheek and smiled.

"Please tell us that Julie fell to her death," Savannah begged.

Craig stared into her face. "Would it make this any easier for you?"

Savannah dropped her head. "No, probably not," she said.

"So what do you think happened?" Michael asked.

Craig tightened his lips into a thin line. "We'll know for sure after the autopsy, but I think she was dead before she went out the window."

"Good lord," Michael said. "So what did you find out during your interrogations?"

The detective glanced at Michael and then Savannah. "Well, I haven't talked to either of you, yet." He flipped open his notebook. "…but here's what I know so far, Lance heard someone come up the stairs in the middle of the night. Cheryl said she didn't leave her room all night, except once, to get a drink of water in the kitchen. And she thought she heard scuffling on the second floor above her. DeeDee heard something outside their bedroom door, but when she went to take a look, all she saw was your cat. Raymond slept through everything and so did Rob. Neither Rob nor Lance were aware if the other one had gotten up in the night. Both of them said they slept like logs."

"And the two guys outside; did they see or hear anything?" Savannah asked.

"Naw, I doubt it. If they did, they ain't talkin'."

Michael stood. "I'm thirsty. Anyone want a glass of tea or water?"

"Tea sounds great," Craig said, following Michael toward the kitchen. "Thanks."

Savannah stood and began picking up the trays of fruit and sweet rolls.

"Let me help," Craig said, as he reached for a tray of small paper plates, silverware, and napkins. Michael stopped at the buffet on his way into the kitchen and snagged as many coffee cups as he could carry.

"Thanks, guys," Savannah said. She set the trays on the counter and headed back into the living room for Lily.

Michael stepped closer to the large kitchen window. "Looks like the film crew is getting ready to leave," he said. He turned to Craig. "Okay if they leave town?"

Craig nodded. "I know where to find them."

Just then, they heard a rap on the door. Michael called out, "It's Maggie and Max."

"I wondered how long it would take her to get over here," Savannah said as she placed the cradle swing next to the table in the kitchen. "She never misses a party…" She choked up. "...or a tragedy."

"Michael, what happened?" Margaret asked as she rushed through the door. "I saw all the cop cars." She gasped in a panic, "The baby's okay, isn't she?"

"She's fine," Michael assured her. "We're all fine."

"Well, when I opened the drapes and saw the emergency vehicles, I got scared. I made Max come over here with me."

"I told her someone probably partied too hearty," Max said.

Michael nodded. "Something like that."

"Oh hi, Craig. We aren't intruding are we?" Margaret asked as she rushed to where Lily lay sleeping. She lowered her voice. "Oh there you are, precious baby. You *are* all right." She leaned over and kissed Lily on the forehead. "So what did you say, Craig?"

"I said, you're not intruding; in fact, maybe you can shed some light on what happened here last night."

"What did happen?" she asked, her bobbed hair swaying slightly as she looked from Craig to Savannah to Michael."

"Let me take your coats. Coffee's still hot. Help yourself to some fruit there on the counter," Savannah said.

Margaret slipped out of her maroon fleece jacket and handed it to Savannah. Max hung his black windbreaker over a chair back. Once the pair each had a cup of coffee in their hands and were seated at the table, Margaret said, "Well, we don't have all day."

"What she means is, she doesn't have much patience," Max said quietly.

"You got that right," Savannah said with a forced smile.

Craig placed a piece of pineapple on a small plate and sat down across from Margaret. "Well, we may have a murder on our hands, or…"

"Murder!" Margaret said with a gasp. "Who? How?"

Savannah was quick to respond. "Someone was pushed out an upstairs window," she said solemnly, near tears.

"They don't know that for sure," Michael explained.

"Who?" Margaret asked.

"Do you remember Julie?" Craig asked.

"The chunky gal? Oh yes," Margaret said. She gave Craig a piercing stare. "Did Cheryl do it?"

Craig sat forward in his chair. "Now why do you say that, Maggie?"

"Because those two gals hated each other. Didn't you notice that last night?"

"I saw them going at it yesterday afternoon, too," Michael said.

"Fighting?" Craig asked.

Michael shook his head. "Naw, I guess you'd say arguing…loudly."

"Well, they were fighting at the party," Margaret said, her eyes wide with excitement. "…or just about to."

Craig made notes. "What were they arguing about?" he asked.

Margaret and Michael looked at each other. She shrugged. "I don't know. They were just hissing at each other like a couple of wildcats."

"Rob had to break them up," Michael added. "Didn't you see that yesterday, Craig?"

He shook his head. "I think I was outside then. Iris said something about it."

"And to think I was going to put them in the same room last night," Savannah said.

"Well, maybe that bombshell Cheryl visited Julie after lights out and tossed her out the window…or Julie jumped out the window to get away from her," Margaret said, not cracking a smile.

"Do you think they hated each other that much?" Craig asked.

Margaret thinned her lips and stared off into space. "That's hard to say. Who knows what another person is capable of? I don't know anything about any of those people."

"Well, what about Lance, Auntie?" Savannah asked. "Don't you know him?"

Margaret grew silent. She looked down at her hands in her lap and fidgeted with the hem of her loose-fitting blouse. She looked up at Savannah and glanced toward Max. She took a deep breath and said, "Yeah, I know him. I dated him once."

"Dated him?" Savannah said. "Isn't he a lot…"

"Younger than me?" Margaret snapped. "Yes. I was widowed, lonely, and vulnerable." She paused and then continued, "He was…well, available." She smirked when she said, "He was always available."

"He appears to be a nice-enough guy," Max said. "I had a conversation with him last night about feral cats. He seemed genuinely interested."

Margaret put her hand on Max's arm. "Oh, Max, you don't know. You just don't know."

"Is something wrong with him?" he asked. "You sound kind of frightened of him."

"No, not really frightened. I don't think he's dangerous. He's just the love-'em-and-leave-'em type, if you know what I mean."

Everyone stared in Margaret's direction, waiting for more. Except for Michael, who shot a concerned look in Savannah's direction.

"Did he break your heart?" Craig asked.

Margaret thought about the question and then answered, "Well, yeah, he kinda did." She looked up at the inquiring faces around her. "And he didn't even seem to remember me."

Savannah reached out and touched her aunt's hand. "Gosh, Auntie, he really hurt you, didn't he?"

Margaret let out a laugh. "Yeah, me and every other available woman in town…and some that weren't."

"Weren't what?" Craig asked. "Available? You mean he's a ladies' man and he goes after married women, too?" He made a couple of notes.

"You might say that," Margaret agreed.

"He does know how to turn on the charm," Savannah said.

"Yeah, he had Savannah cornered here in the kitchen last night, wanting to take nude pictures of her," Michael spat.

"Michael," Savannah complained.

"Well, didn't he?" he challenged.

Savannah sat back and nodded.

"Oh no, Vannie. He came on to you?" She tightened her lips and said, "That dirty, no-good..."

"It's okay, Auntie," she said looking adoringly at her husband. "Michael took care of the situation."

"Yeah, he's charming—likable," Margaret said. She leaned toward Savannah and continued, "But Vannie, there is something wrong with that man…something terribly wrong."

"Wow, I've never seen you like this, Auntie. He really got to you."

"Is he capable of murder?" Craig asked bluntly.

The room became quiet as everyone waited for Margaret's response. Finally she shook her head and said, "Gosh, I'm no psychologist…"

"Yeah, but you have an opinion," Craig urged. "What do you think? What is your gut feeling?"

Rap-rap.

"Oh, come on in, Rob," Michael said, when he saw the producer through the window in the kitchen door.

"Just want to thank you all for your hospitality," Rob said, waving a hand at the group at the table. "I'll be in touch."

Everyone waved and bid Rob farewell. Michael walked over and shook the man's hand. He stood at the door watching as the film crew made final preparations to leave. "Well, I'll be," Michael said.

"What?" Margaret and Savannah asked. He had the attention of the two men, as well.

"I just saw Lance and Cheryl in a lip-lock and then she climbed into his car with him." He turned to face the others. "I didn't know they were a couple."

"No, I didn't either," Savannah said. "Did you see that coming, Craig?"

"Nope. There was no indication of it when I talked to everyone earlier."

"Well, that's Lance Grayson for you," Margaret said. "Killer? I don't think so, but he's going to take every opportunity to get what he wants, and Cheryl is the kind of thing he always wants."

"I thought he and Julie were an item," Savannah said. "Didn't you see the way she was latched onto him last night?" As Craig took more notes, Savannah continued. "Yeah, that was the message I got from Julie, anyway—that those two were dating."

"When it comes to Lance Grayson," Margaret said, "everyone's his date at one time or another."

The room grew silent for a few moments. While the others sipped coffee or took a bite of their food, Michael looked at his wife; concern on his face.

***

The following evening around six, Michael returned home from work. "Did you see the paper, hon?" he asked when he saw Savannah sitting on the sofa, her Kindle on her lap.

"Yes, I read it while Lily napped. We're in the news again, aren't we?" She grimaced. "I just hate that this happened here."

Michael sat on the sofa next to Savannah and wrapped his arms around her. He held her for a few moments before proceeding with his evening ritual. "I guess they've determined she was murdered," he said, removing his sport shoes and socks.

Savannah ran her fingertips gently up and down Michael's back. "Yeah, that wasn't an easy pill to swallow," she said.

He leaned forward and relaxed his body, mumbling, "Mmmm, feels good." After a few moments, he sat straight and faced her. "I wonder if they have any suspects."

"Looks like Cheryl is the strongest one," she said.

He grinned at her. "Is that what Rags told you?"

She looked confused. "Rags?"

"Yeah, has he dug up evidence to that effect?"

"I don't think so," she said. "And I hope he doesn't. I just want this to go away."

Michael looked at Savannah for a moment. He took her hand and began massaging it between his fingers and thumb. She squeezed his hand and said, "It looks like Colbi and Damon's friends are okay."

Michael frowned. "Friends?"

"Colbi was concerned about some of the homeless people they know living down near the river. You remember, they got to know a couple of them when they were working on the story about the homeless gal who was living in that shed behind our property last year. There were rumors that some of them disobeyed evacuation orders. Damon's story said three men had to be rescued, but everyone got out safely. I guess their camp was washed away, though. That whole area was flooded."

"Sounds like quite a nightmare. I wonder where they went to get out of the weather."

"According to the story, a local church took in those who wanted shelter. I suppose the others just took cover in abandoned outsheds, empty dumpsters, unlocked cars, and under canopies."

Michael stared at his wife. "You sure have a good imagination."

"No, that's what they do, Michael. Some of them sleep in old abandoned cardboard boxes for shelter. But I guess not in the rain."

"How do you know what the homeless do?" he asked.

She pulled back from him a little and put her hand on one hip. "Don't you read stories about the homeless? I find them interesting. I just finished a novel about a homeless couple. They lived under a bridge." She laughed. "Like trolls. Only you can't safely live under a bridge when it's flooding."

"Hmmm," Michael murmured. "Hey, let's change the subject, shall we?" he suggested. "How was your day? Did you do anything special?"

She smiled. "Every day is special with our daughter. She's such a sweetie."

"Where is she, napping?"

"No. Actually, she's on a playdate," Savannah said with a grin.

Michael stiffened his posture. "What?" he all but demanded.

"Well, I had a few errands to run and Iris talked me into letting Lily come stay with her and Craig for a while. She practically begged me to be gone for at least two hours. She thought I needed a break." She looked at Michael imploringly. "Michael, my arms ache for my baby."

He chuckled and took his wife in his arms. "You're such a good mommy. But we really should take advantage of help when we can get it. We may want to go someplace without Lily sometime, and we'll need a babysitter." He looked at his watch. "So is two hours up yet?"

Savannah turned his wrist so she could see the time. She sat upright. "Ten more minutes. Let's go get our baby."

"Yes, let's," Michael said, pulling his flip-flops out from under the sofa and slipping them on. "Did Helena come today?" he asked, as he stood and put on a lightweight fleece-lined jacket.

"Yes, we got the beds changed and bathrooms cleaned. I'm glad to have that done. I was creeped out when we were working in Adam's room." When Savannah returned from their bedroom with her jacket, she said, "Michael, I'd like to switch Adam to another room. Can we move him to the blue room?" She frowned. "I really don't want to think of him in that room anymore. How do you feel about it?"

"Yeah, I've been thinking about that." He took a deep breath. "Yes, let's do take him out of there—at least for now. We won't mention anything about what happened. We'll just present him with a new room."

"Good, I like that idea," Savannah said, picking up her purse and heading for the front door. She stopped and said, "You know, I'd really like to have him downstairs with us. Are you up for diving into the unfinished room downstairs for him?"

Michael opened the door and the couple walked out. Before they reached their SUV, he said,

"Yeah. I'd actually like to start another project." He looked at Savannah, a twinkle in his eye. "Maybe Adam would like to help me with this one."

"Gonna teach your son how to make sawdust, huh?" she said.

They both laughed as they entered the car and buckled up.

"Oh, by the way, Michael," she said reaching out and touching his arm. "Charlotte's coming over this evening. Reba has a meeting…or maybe it's a date. Little Ruby is with her dad, and I told Reba that Charlotte could have dinner with us. So we need to be back by seven."

Eight minutes later, the Iveys walked up the pathway to where Iris Clampton lived with her three sons—Damon, and two younger boys, who had been left in her custody by her second husband. Just before they could ring the bell, Brett stepped out through the front doorway. "Oh hello, Dr. Ivey… Savannah…" he said.

"Hi Brett, where are you going in such a hurry?" Michael asked.

Brett, a strapping sixteen-year-old, winked and said, "I have a date."

"Way to go, buddy," Michael said. "Where are you taking her?"

"Uh…a movie downtown."

"The drive-in?" he teased.

"The what?" Brett asked

"Drive-in movie. Aren't there drive-in movies anymore?"

Brett looked confused. "I don't think so. Do you mean like a drive-through at McDonalds?"

"Not quite, Brett," Savannah said. She patted him on the chest and said, "You go on and have fun. Michael can explain drive-in theaters to you another time."

"Uh, thanks, will do," he said.

"You look nice," Savannah called after him as he jogged toward the family car.

Just then, Iris opened the door and called out, "Drive safely, Son." She was startled to see Michael and Savannah heading up the walkway. "Oh, hi. Come for your little girl already?"

"Yup, playdate's over," Michael said with a grin.

"Bummer," she said. "We were having fun." She motioned toward the front door. "Come in, come in." She then called out, "Lily, your folks are here."

As the couple stepped in, they saw Craig sitting on the sofa cradling Lily in one arm and dangling a set of plastic keys in the other hand. "Hi, watch this," he said.

Michael and Savannah watched as Craig lowered the keys and let Lily grab one of them in a pudgy hand. "Hand-eye coordination," he said with a grin. "She's going to be a good shot when she becomes a detective."

"A detective?!" Savannah screeched. "I don't think so."

"What's wrong with being a detective?" Craig asked, as if hurt.

Iris laughed. "Craig, that's not the first choice of careers most parents consider for their little girls. Savannah and Michael probably want to see her become a veterinarian or a doctor."

"Well, the world is wide-open to her," Craig said. "She can become whatever she wants. Right?"

"Yes," Michael said, sitting down in a chair near where Craig sat. He reached over and caressed Lily's chubby leg. "Whatever she wants." He grinned mischievously and said, "Builder, President of the United States…"

"Wife and mother…" Savannah added.

"Dull," Iris said.

"Being a wife and mother is dull?" Savannah challenged. "Not for this wife and mother. I've never been happier."

Michael smiled broadly. He then leaned toward Craig. "Anything new in your investigation? I see that poor Julie was murdered. How did it happen?"

"Awww, I can't talk about stuff like that while I'm holding this angel," he said.

"Then I'll take her," Iris said. She held her hands out. "Gimme, gimme."

"Iris, I don't think I've ever seen you dressed like that," Savannah said.

"Like this?" Iris questioned, looking down at her faded jeans and tie-dyed t-shirt.

"Never. You're such a fashionista."

Iris shrugged. "These are my playdate duds."

"You still look fabulous."

Iris's face brightened. "Well, thanks."

Savannah walked over to where Craig and Michael sat. "So, what can you tell us?" she asked.

Craig cleared his throat. "Julie was with a man sometime before she died. It will be easy enough to find out who."

Savannah gasped. "So a man killed her?"

Craig shook his head. "Not necessarily. We don't even know if she fell or was pushed through the window. She may have been lured to that spot and killed there or her body was dumped there. We can't be sure yet."

"I hope so," Savannah said under her breath.

"Why?" Craig asked.

Michael also waited for her response.

Savannah choked up when she said, "I don't want that kind of negativity connected to Adam's room." Her voice raised an octave. "I don't even like hearing that someone was—you know, being frisky in there."

Michael stood and put his arms around his wife. She wiped at her eyes and apologized to Iris and Craig.

"Hey, you have every right to be upset," Craig said. "This is an awful thing to have happen in your home."

"Yeah," Savannah said, pulling away from Michael, "and to think we were entertaining a killer." She shook her head in disbelief. "It just makes me so mad."

Iris spoke up. "Maybe it wasn't someone you know."

Michael stared at her. "What? Are you suggesting that someone broke into our house that night?"

"Or Julie let someone in," Craig added.

"Are you serious?" Michael asked.

Savannah stood poised to hear Craig's answer.

"Uh, well, we gotta look at all the angles. Anything's possible." Craig took in a deep breath and let it out. "The clues are few and far between at this point. But this case is my priority. We should have some answers soon."

***

Michael, Savannah, and Lily had been home for only a few minutes when Charlotte arrived exactly on time. She waved goodbye to her mom and stepped inside at Savannah's invitation.

"Whereth Ragth?" the teen asked.

"He's waiting for his dinner. Would you like to help me feed the animals?"

"The horth, too?" she asked excitedly.

"Peaches is still boarded at Bonnie's place. Guess who's her next-door neighbor."

"Who?" Charlotte asked.

"Wilson."

"I love that horth. He goeth thlow for me. When can I ride Wilthon again?"

Savannah put her hand on the teen's shoulder. "Soon," she said. "We really should do that and very soon."

Once the cats and dog were fed and the humans had eaten, Charlotte asked if she and Rags could go upstairs and play in Adam's room.

"Sure. We'll clean up the kitchen and then we'll be in the nursery getting Lily ready for bed."

"Ohhhh," Charlotte said. "I want to help."

Savannah looked at Michael and then back at Charlotte. "Okay, you go play with Rags while we clean the kitchen and we'll call you when it's time to put the baby to bed."

"Okay!" Charlotte said. "Come on Ragth. Let'th go play," she called as she headed for the staircase.

Thirty minutes later, Michael and Savannah were on the floor playing with Lily when they spotted Charlotte walking carefully down the stairs. Rags bounded after her.

"Doeth Buffy like the baby?" Charlotte asked, as she approached them.

Savannah looked over at the cat, who was lying in a meatloaf position on an edge of Lily's blanket. "Yes she does. They're buddies."

"Hi Buffy," Charlotte said, plopping down next to her. She began petting the cat's plush coat. "Thee'th purring," she said. "Ragth doethen't purr very loud."

"No he doesn't," Michael said. "Buffy has a loud motor and Rags's is quiet."

"Thee hath a motor?" Charlotte asked, eyes wide.

Savannah laughed. "He's joking. It's not really a motor. It just sounds like a motor."

"Oh," Charlotte said, looking confused.

"So what did you two play upstairs?" Savannah asked.

Charlotte sat straight. "Rags has some new things," she reported

"New things?" Savannah questioned rather casually.

"Yeah, in hith toy bokth."

"Like what?" Michael asked.

"I'll thow you," she said rising to her feet and heading up the stairs, Rags on her heels.

When the pair returned, Charlotte held out her hands and displayed a stick of gum still in the wrapper, a used tea bag, an axle and wheels off one of Adam's toy cars, a plastic bag containing hearing-aid batteries, and a small silk scarf with a floral design printed on it.

Savannah and Michael chuckled when they saw the array of items Charlotte had retrieved. "Crazy cat!" Michael exclaimed.

"Uh-oh, someone's going to need these hearing-aid batteries," Savannah said. She thought for a moment and then said, "I think Glenda Cathcart wears a hearing aid."

Michael reached out for the car wheels. "Adam was looking for this last time he was here," he said.

Suddenly, Savannah gasped. "Oh, Michael, that's Cheryl's scarf. She had it tied around her neck on Saturday."

"How do you suppose Rags got his paws on it?" he asked.

"I don't know, but we'd better call Craig."

"Do you think it's a clue? Wait…are you saying you think Cheryl went in there and…?"

"I don't know!" Savannah said, sounding near hysterics. When she noticed a look of panic on Charlotte's pretty face, she calmed down some. She reached up and squeezed the girl's hand. "I'm sorry, sweetie," She said. "Everything's okay. I didn't mean to upset you." She smiled at the girl. "Look, Lily's rubbing her eyes. You know what that means, don't you?"

Charlotte blinked a couple of times. "Um, thee'th thleepy?"

"That's right. Shall we get her ready for bed?"

"Yeth," she said, her demeanor improving considerably.

***

By the time Savannah and Michael waved goodbye to Charlotte and Reba, it was nearly eight-thirty. "Thank you for helping with Lily," Savannah called after Charlotte.

"Thank you for entertaining my girl," Reba said, hugging her daughter to her as they stepped out to their car.

"It's not too late to call Craig, is it?" Savannah asked as she closed the front door and locked it.

Michael looked at his watch. "Naw, I'm sure it isn't. So what are you going to tell him?"

"That we found possible evidence of Cheryl's involvement in Julie's…death," she said.

He squinted his eyes. "Uh, wait a minute there, Sherlock. Cheryl may not have gone anywhere near that room. It could be that Rags took the scarf out of her room downstairs and carried it up to his stash. There's no way of knowing how it actually got there."

Savannah stopped and thought about it. "But the bedroom doors were closed during the night—I'm pretty certain of that. I suggested that everyone close their doors to keep the cats out. So Rags probably didn't actually have access to the bedrooms that night."

"Unless someone got up to use the restroom and left their door open for a moment. Rags can be fast," Michael said.

"And sneaky," Savannah added.

"Yes, and we know that Cheryl went into the kitchen for a glass of water at some point during the night, or so she says."

"Or the murderer might have planted the scarf in Julie's room and investigators thought it was Julie's, so they overlooked it as evidence…or they didn't see it."

Michael pushed back the stubborn, straight hairs that hung over one side of his forehead. "Okay," he said, "I can see that Craig needs to know about this find. I'm glad I don't have to work with that piece of evidence. It's a puzzle to me."

"And maybe just the puzzle piece Craig needs," Savannah said as she made the call.

***

The following morning, Michael appeared at the doorway to the nursery. "Who are you talking to in here?" he asked, a big grin on his face.

"Hi hon," Savannah said. "Lily and I are having a conversation."

"About what?" he asked as he joined his wife at the changing table. "Or is it girlie stuff?"

"I'm not sure," Savannah said. "I think she's just expressing her joy on this beautiful day." She chuckled. "She sounds like a pigeon."

Michael frowned. "Pigeon?"

"Yeah, I think it's pigeon talk… 'Coo, coo.'"

"Pigeon talk?" Michael said. "That's funny."

Just then, Lily let out a sweet cooing sound. Michael smiled down at his daughter. "She *does* sound like a pigeon—a baby pigeon." He looked serious for a moment and then said, "Although, I don't think I've ever heard a baby pigeon coo, have you?"

"Can't say that I have."

Mew.

"Hi Buffy, time to get up, huh, girl?" Savannah said, reaching out and running her hand over the cat's plush fur.

MEOW

"Here comes the big guy," Michael said, lifting Lily off the changing table. "Do you see the kitties?" he asked the baby. "There's Buffy and Rags…"

"It's a wonder her first sounds aren't cat-like," Savannah said with a laugh.

"Right," Michael agreed. "Mews, instead of coos."

"So what's on your agenda today?" he asked Savannah.

"Rags and I are going to a classroom at Pleasant Acres School this afternoon."

"Oh, your therapy program?"

"Yes, Janice and I will introduce the program to students and teachers."

"You're really getting into this, aren't you?" he said.

"Yes, are you okay with it?"

"Are you enjoying it?" he asked.

"I am. I'm not sure I want to get more deeply involved, but I would like to help launch a program that's ongoing in this and other communities."

"And where are you going today, my pigeon princess?" he asked, looking down at Lily.

"She's going to spend some time with Colbi and Damon. Colbi is so excited, only…"

Michael frowned. "Only what?"

"Only I'm afraid Lily will be with them during her regular naptime. She may not be very entertaining." She looked over at Michael's watch. "Hey, let's get you some breakfast. You have to go to work this morning, right?"

"Sure do. We have a busy week ahead. I'll even be seeing a couple of horses." Michael walked out into the hallway with Lily and then turned and asked, "Hey, what did Craig say about the scarf Rags found?"

"Not much. He'll come by and get it. He isn't sure how important it is…unless…"

"Unless what?"

"Well, unless the bedroom doors were closed."

"Yeah, I guess that's a pivotal point, isn't it? Have you asked Rags?"

"Funny," Savannah said with a smirk. "So what time will you be home this evening?" she asked.

"Do we have plans?"

"No, just want to make sure Lily and I are home by then."

"Actually, I think Damon and I are going to the library after work," Michael said

"Really? Why?"

"We're interested in those stairs and that wall."

Savannah grinned at her husband. "You just can't let that mystery go, can you?"

"Not when it's so illogical." He chuckled. "It's interesting how fascinated Damon is with it."

"So what are you two going to do?"

"Glenda has given me permission to break into the wall and find out why it's constructed that way." He looked at Savannah. "You know, it really isn't a safe situation—stairs are a fascination for kids. Someone could get hurt. In fact, Glenda said that a child fell into that stairwell once and got a bloody nose. The library doesn't need a lawsuit."

"What time do you think you'll be finished?" Savannah asked, while pouring them each a glass of juice.

"Maybe by six."

"How about we have dinner at the diner tonight? Mexican food's the special."

"Sounds good." He looked down at Lily in his arms and said, "Do you like enchiladas and tacos?"

She waved her arms and smiled.

"I think that's a 'yes,'" he said, laughing.

***

It was nearly five that afternoon when Michael pulled up in front of the library and parked his veterinary truck. "Hi there," he greeted as he saw Damon appear through a slot in the hedge surrounding the parking lot. "I hear you've been entertained by our child this afternoon."

Damon's smile widened. "Yes, we were. She is something else, you know it?" He lowered his head and chuckled. "Of course, you do."

"So what did you guys do?"

"Oh, we stared at her a lot. Colbi read her a story. We played peek-a-boo, five-little-piggies and, oh, she really enjoyed watching Dolly play. We'd toss a toy and Dolly would run after it. Lily would just giggle up a storm. Yes, she entertained us, all right." He punched Michael in the arm and said, "Thanks for sharing."

"She giggled?" Michael asked.

"Well, it sounded like giggling to me. She was happy."

"Glad you showed her a good time," he said. "She probably has more adult friends than most kids." Michael patted Damon on the back. "She's the luckiest girl ever." Michael, flashlight in hand, reached into a compartment in the back of his veterinary truck and pulled out a drill. "Hey, let's go check out this situation."

"We're really going to drill into that wall?" Damon asked.

"I think we are," Michael said, leading the way into the library.

The secret garden area was empty when they arrived. First Michael knocked on the wall. "There's more of an echo—hollow sound—down low than up high. Did you notice that?" he asked.

"Yeah—it does sound different. Why's that?"

"I'm not sure yet, but we're about to find out. Let's drill here," he suggested, marking a spot about two feet up from the bottom step. Once he had created a hole about three inches in diameter, Michael said, "Hand me that flashlight, will ya?"

Damon moved closer to where Michael stood and watched as he shined the light through the hole. Michael squatted down and peered in, aiming the flashlight at all angles. "Well, there are the rest of the steps," he said, looking down to his left. He pulled away from the hole and handed Damon the light. "Take a look—there's definitely a room down there, just like Maggie remembers."

"Well, I'll be," Damon said. "They left furniture and shelves with stuff still on them. But why?"

"That's I'd like to know," Michael said. "It's the craziest thing I've ever seen." He shook his head. "I mean, if they did this to protect kids from falling down the stairs, why leave some stairs exposed?"

Damon turned to face Michael. He creased his brow. "Maybe the secret garden really does hold a secret."

Michael grinned. "You sound like some kind of reporter…or novelist," he said.

Damon laughed. "Hey, I couldn't make up a story like this." In a more serious tone, he said, "But I'd like to know more about it, wouldn't you? Do you think they'd let us tear this wall out?"

Michael narrowed his lips. "I think it would be a good idea, actually."

"How so?" Damon asked.

"Well, as I said, that small stairwell needs to be made safer."

Just then, Glenda stepped into the courtyard. "How's it going out here?" she asked.

"Come look," Michael invited. "Damon, give her that flashlight, would you? Now, it's a little awkward to see in, so you may have to kneel down there. Here, you can sit on my jacket."

"Oh my," she said as she peered in through the hole. "That's odd. I mean, I knew this room was here, but I guess I thought it had been removed—not just walled over. It appears to be still intact, doesn't it?"

"Sure does," Damon said. "There are games, books, furniture, and things down there. And what's up with that light?"

"Light? What light?" Michael and Glenda asked.

"Didn't you see the light on the far side of the room?"

Michael frowned. "I didn't see a light. Do you see one, Glenda?"

"I think you can see it better without the flashlight," Damon suggested.

Glenda jumped a little. "Yes! There it is. I see a small red glow, like a point on a laser beam." She sat up and looked at Damon. "Is that what you saw?"

He nodded. "That's it. What do you suppose it is?" he asked.

Glenda took a deep breath. "I don't have a clue."

"Here, let me see." Michael helped Glenda up, then knelt down and peered through the hole. "By gosh, there is a light on down there. But my flashlight doesn't shine far enough for me to see what it's attached to." He shook his head. "Someone must have been in an awful hurry to get this job done, if they left something plugged in."

"What do you suggest?" Glenda asked, looking from Michael to Damon.

Michael thought about it for a moment and asked, "Damon, would you like some real-life experience as a builder?"

His eyes widened. "Sure! You mean you and me…?"

"Why not?" Michael said. He turned to Glenda. "Would it be okay if Damon and I work up a bid for you to take down this wall? You'll be able to get into that room and see if anything you need was left in there. We can unplug whatever it is that's running up your electric bill and we can build a new wall that encloses the entire staircase with a door or a gate you can lock."

"Yeah," Damon said, "but why not utilize the space instead of wall it off like this?"

"We can sure use the extra room," Glenda said. "Patrons often come to us asking to rent space for their meetings and events. It could create additional revenue for the library. And storage is a problem. If we cleaned out some areas in the main library and moved the stuff down here, we could relinquish a room in the main library for community use." She clasped her hands together under her chin. "Oh yes, I'd love to have access to that room." She then looked up at Michael. "Sure. Write up a bid—let's do it!" she said. "I'll put in a good word for you with the board."

***

Michael arrived home shortly after six and found Savannah feeding Lily. "Hi hon," she said. "We'll be ready in a few minutes."

He leaned down and kissed Savannah and then Lily. "Good, that'll give me time to wash up."

They met at the front door, jackets and baby in hand at six-fifteen. Michael slipped on his jacket and then reached for Lily. "So how did it go with your school visit?"

"Really well," Savannah said, heaving the diaper bag strap over one shoulder, "only…"

"Uh-oh. What happened?" he asked when he saw the playful grin on her face.

"Well…" She started to laugh. "Rags…" She laughed harder.

"You don't need to tell me any more," he said, shaking his head. "What did he do, eat the kids' crayons, steal their homework, leap from a top shelf onto the teacher's shoulder?"

Savannah was doubled over with laughter by now. "No," she said between chortles. "You'd never guess this one," she said laughing out loud. She took a few breaths in an attempt to curb her hysterics and said, "Actually, it didn't strike me as this funny at the time, but…" Before she could tell Michael the story, she burst out laughing again.

"Tsk, tsk," Michael said. "Let's get you into the car, giggles, before you bust a gut." He murmured to the baby on the way out the door, "Don't mind Mommy, she's having a giggle-fest."

"Okay, Michael, I think I can tell you the story now," Savannah said from the backseat of their SUV. "He…" She laughed again, then cleared her throat. "Well, these kids were passing a note, and he…he…he intercepted it."

Michael was laughing at Savannah's inability to stop laughing. Then he said, "You're right. It isn't that funny."

She leaned forward. "Yeah, unless you were there to see what happened next. This little girl, Jessica, was handing a note to the girl in front of her. I think her name was Kaylie, and she dropped it. Rags saw this and he ran over and picked it up. Jessica let out a scream—well, more of a squeal—and everyone turned to look at her. In the meantime, Rags ran to the back of the classroom with the note and dropped it at the feet of a boy named Reggie. All eyes were on Reggie. He leaned over and picked up the note. By now, Jessica is practically hyperventilating, she's so upset."

"What's the teacher doing while all this is going on?" Michael asked.

"Well, I was about to tell you. She sees what has happened and she heads for Reggie, I guess to retrieve the note, and that's when Rags spots something interesting on a table in the back of the room." She laughs again. "Michael, they have a rat in a cage. He's a class mascot or something."

"Oh no," Michael said. "Don't tell me, Rags had him for lunch."

"Not quite. So he jumps up on the table next to the rat and goes eye-to-eye with him. Before we could react, Rags bats the little cage off the table, the door opens, and the rat scurries out across the room just as the teacher is heading for that note. Most of the girls are screaming and climbing up on their desks. Some of the boys take off after the rat and the cat. In the process, somehow a vase of flowers gets knocked over and the water spills out just as Rags is running under the teacher's desk after the rat."

Now Michael is laughing. "It spilled on Rags?"

"Yes! It was a big vase full of water and…" she started laughing uncontrollably again. "…he was soaked," she said, trying to catch her breath. "So the rat disappears under the teacher's desk, but he comes out on the other side and two of the boys are able to corner it and put it away. The girls come down off their desks and now everyone is wondering where the cat is."

"Where was he," Michael asked, still laughing, "licking his wounds?"

"Pretty much. When I pulled him out from under the teacher's desk, he looked like a drenched rat. There was water running off his forehead, his ears were kind of sideways, and the kids were all laughing at him. He slinked over to the carrier, went inside, and spent the next half hour licking himself dry."

"Oh, poor Rags," Michael said. "How humiliating for him. So what happened to the note?" he asked.

"Well, Jessica, I think, would have liked to crawl into the carrier with Rags, she was so embarrassed. The note she passed was about Reggie. She was mortified when Rags took it to him, of all people."

"Did he read it? What did it say?"

"Yeah, during Rags's little melee, the teacher became distracted and she rushed over to clean up the flower spill. When things settled down, the boy sitting next to Reggie urged him to read the note. He didn't reveal the contents, but it was obvious what was in it. He blushed and Jessica made a quick exit from the room." Savannah settled down in her seat and said, "I don't think Jessica will be passing notes in class again anytime soon."

"No, I would imagine not," Michael said. "So Rags didn't make a very good impression as a reading therapy cat, did he?"

"Actually, he couldn't have been better. In a little while, after Reggie's blush had faded, Jessica had returned to her desk, and Rags had cleaned himself up, our cat performed quite well. He didn't go near that rat cage again, I'll tell you that."

"We're here. Hon, you must be famished after the day you had."

"Yeah, and tired," she said as she climbed out of the car.

When the couple entered the diner, Michael carrying Lily in her infant seat, Iris greeted them. "Hi," she said, gravitating toward Lily. "How's my sweet girl?" she cooed. Lily smiled up at her.

"So what brings you out?" she asked.

"Hunger," Michael said with a grin. He spotted a booth across the room and said, "Okay if we sit over there?"

"Sure," Iris said. "Wherever you want."

Michael slid the baby seat into the booth against the wall and started to scoot in next to her.

"Wait, I want to sit with her," Savannah said.

"You rode next to her in the car and I haven't seen her all day," he protested.

"I was gone from her today, too," she said.

"You two are hilarious," Iris said, laughing. "Most parents argue over who *has* to get up with the baby."

"They do?" Michael asked.

"Yes, they do," she said in all seriousness. She pointed at Michael. "Now why don't you sit next to her while eating your dinner and switch with Savannah during dessert."

The couple stared at her for a minute and then looked at each other, nodded, and slid into their seats.

"That's better," Iris said with a chuckle. "We don't want any domestic disturbances here. Now, what can I get you to drink?"

"Herbal iced tea," Savannah said.

Michael nodded. "Same for me."

"Well, look who's here," Iris said, just before walking away.

Michael twisted around in his seat. "Hi Craig," he said, reaching out to shake the detective's hand. "How're things?"

"Good. Just out for a bite to eat before I call it a night." He winked at Savannah and said to Michael, "Couldn't you get her to cook one of her delicious meals for you tonight?"

"Oh we've both been on the run all day. Decided to let someone serve us this evening." He motioned to Craig, "Hey, why don't you join us; we haven't ordered yet."

Craig glanced at Savannah again. "Sure, if you don't mind."

"We'd love to have you," she said as she scooted over to make room for him. "So how's the investigation going?" she asked.

"Slow. But that's not unusual for a case like this." He turned toward Savannah and said, "Thanks for letting me know about that scarf, by the way. I think it's a strong clue."

"Well, yeah, unless…"

"Unless what?" he asked.

Savannah responded, "Unless Rags found it somewhere else in the house and took it into that room later. There's really no way of knowing how Cheryl's scarf ended up in Julie's room."

"Yeah, I know. But there's other evidence pointing to Cheryl, as well."

Michael and Savannah waited to hear more.

"As you know, the two women didn't get along; and Cheryl has a history."

"Yeah, we know about the fighting. But a history?" Michael asked. "What kind of history?"

"She's been arrested for violent acts before. She's a strong suspect."

"She's quite a bit smaller than Julie was. Do you think she could toss her out the window?" Savannah asked.

"She's into bodybuilding," Craig said.

"Hi babe," Iris said when she approached the booth with two iced teas and a coffee. She looked around and then bent over and kissed Craig.

"Hi yourself," he said. "What's for dinner?"

"Anything you want," she said with a smile. "The special is fajitas. I've heard people say it's pretty good tonight."

"That's what I'll have," Michael said.

"Sounds good," Savannah agreed.

"Yup, me too," Craig said.

Iris nodded. "You make my job so easy. Three fajitas it is."

"So Craig, you say she lifts weights?" Michael said. "I didn't notice she had that kind of muscle tone."

Savannah smirked across the table at her husband. "Yeah, that's because the cleavage caught your eye."

Michael squirmed a little in his seat. "Now, that's not…"

Craig winked. "Come on Michael, she's got you there. How could you notice anything but?"

"Plus, she wore a jacket most of the time," Savannah said. "A jacket that didn't cover her plunging neckline." She turned toward Craig. "So are you going to arrest her?"

"We're hoping to have enough evidence soon. We still have to get DNA from Cheryl and the men in the crew." He looked across at Lily. "Enough about me. How are you two and that cute baby?"

"Good," Michael said.

"I talked to Damon earlier and he told me that you might be doing some construction at the library."

Michael leaned forward and rested his elbows on the table. "Yeah. They have a strange situation there. Damon and I drilled a hole in the wall at the bottom of the steps and found a room, just like Maggie remembers as a kid."

"Really? I wonder why they walled it in like that."

"I don't know. But the weirdest thing is—and Savannah, I haven't had a chance to tell you about this yet—there appears to be something plugged in and running down there."

"What?" Craig asked.

"We don't know, but we can see a small light. Something down there is still using electricity."

"How long has the room been boarded up like that?" Craig asked.

"Near as we can figure, about four years. Glenda Cathcart is thrilled at the possibility of opening it up so they can actually use it."

"She didn't know about the room?" Craig asked.

Michael shook his head and squinted. "Well, I guess she knew it was there, but had kind of forgotten about it. She's as eager to learn what mysteries lie beyond that wall as Damon and I are."

Just then Savannah felt her phone vibrate. She looked down at it for a moment, and decided to let the call go to voicemail. She then checked her voicemail messages and was stunned to hear, "Hi Savannah, this is Lance. Just calling to see how you're doing after the shoot. I'll be in town for a few days. Would love to have coffee with you. Call me."

Just as Savannah dropped the phone into her purse, Iris arrived with their order. The two men, who had been deep in conversation, pulled back so she could serve the food and everyone began to eat.

That's odd, Savannah thought. *Why would Lance call me like that? I thought Michael and I made it perfectly clear that I'm not available or interested in anything he has to offer. Well, maybe he'll get the message when he doesn't get a call back from me. At least I hope so,* she thought as she took a bite of her fajita.

Chapter 6

"Hi Auntie," Savannah said when she greeted Margaret at the front door the next morning. "How are you?"

"Great. It's a beautiful morning. I walked over here, you know," she said with pride. She pinched herself around the waist. "I'm determined to get rid of some of this flab."

"Oh, you look good," Savannah said as she closed the door behind her aunt.

"Yeah, not next to you, I don't."

Savannah scowled. "Are we having a competition?"

Margaret looked her niece up and down, sighed, and said, "That train left the station a long time ago. I never did and never will have your height and svelte figure."

"And I'll never have your beautiful skin," Savannah said. "You don't even wrinkle, do you?" she asked, examining her aunt's face more closely.

Margaret brought her hands up to her face and gently patted her cheeks. "Yeah, I guess I do have something going for me."

"Oh Auntie, you're a riot. So do you want a cup of coffee and some low-fat blueberry cobbler?" she asked enticingly.

"Yeowza," Margaret said enthusiastically. She looked around. "Where's the princess?"

"In the kitchen waiting for us," Savannah said, looping her arm through her aunt's. "Let's not keep her waiting."

"Certainly not," Margaret said as the two of them walked toward the kitchen.

"Hi Buffy," Margaret said, bending down to pet the little cat. "Are you keeping Lily company?"

Savannah smiled down at the cat. "She thinks Lily is her very own baby."

"What about the bad boy? Does he show much interest in her?"

"Not too much," Savannah said, pensively. "But he sure likes her toys! Yesterday morning, I was rushing around getting things done and I heard Lily fuss. I looked over at her and Rags had her toy kitty in his mouth. He was tugging at it trying to get it out of her hand."

"How funny," Margaret said. "So who won the tug-of-war?" she asked with a chuckle.

"Lily. She has quite a grip. She would not let go. I'm always finding her toys in his stash, though. He's incorrigible." She looked over at her aunt. "You can sit next to Lily, if you want. I'll let you dish up your cobbler."

Savannah sat down and had just taken a sip of coffee when the doorbell rang. "Who's that?" she asked frowning. She glanced up at the kitchen clock. "Kind of early for an unexpected guest."

"Probably the religious people," Margaret said.

"Religious people?" Savannah asked, looking confused.

"You know, they come around and talk religion to you."

"Oh," Savannah said as she headed for the front door. When she opened it, she stood stunned. "Uh, what are you doing here?" she asked.

"Was in the neighborhood and thought I'd stop by," the visitor said with a smile. "Can you spare a cup of coffee for a friend on a chilly morning?"

Savannah thought about the request, sighed, and opened the door. "Sure, come in," she said.

"Auntie, you remember Lance Grayson," Savannah said when the two of them entered the kitchen.

"Uh, yes. Hello," Margaret said, shooting a questioning glance at her niece.

Lance's demeanor abruptly changed. "Oh, Maggie. Didn't know you were here," he said.

"Why wouldn't I be?" she challenged. "Vannie *is* my niece." She looked him in the eyes and asked, "What brings you here? I thought you lived up near Frisco."

"I do. But I'm here on business for a few days. Uh…Rob asked me to check in on Savannah to make sure everything's okay after the shoot." He looked squarely at Margaret. "Is that okay with you, Maggie?"

"Sit down, Lance," Savannah invited. "How do you take your coffee?"

"Black is fine," he said, choosing a chair across from Savannah. He looked at her. "So is everything okay after the shoot? There's no damage or anything, is there?"

Savannah shook her head. "I don't think so. It's nice of you to check on us. Tell Rob I appreciate it."

"Sure will."

"When will the documentary air?" Margaret asked.

"And where?" Savannah added.

"I think Rob has to find a sponsor for it. It may be picked up by the animal channel. We might put some of it on YouTube."

"Your cat's going viral, Vannie," Margaret said.

Lance smiled at Savannah. "Vannie. Is that what friends call you?" he asked. "I like it."

"No!" Margaret said. "Just family. I call her that and so does her mother and sister. Otherwise, she's Savannah," she said sternly. She then softened a little and asked, "Can we get a copy?"

"Of what?" Lance asked.

"The documentary," she spouted. "Where's your mind today, Lance?" she asked in a rather accusatory manner.

"Help yourself to the cobbler, Lance," Savannah offered, placing a plate and fork in front of him.

"It's really good," Margaret said, wiping her mouth with a paper napkin. "I'll bet Michael loves it when you cook like this."

Savannah shot her aunt a look. *Why is she acting that way?* she wondered.

"So Vannie, I hear that Michael might tear that wall out at the library," Margaret said.

"Gosh, gossip travels fast in this town," Savannah said. "Who told you that?"

"Does it matter? Is it true? Is he contracting out now as a demolitioner?"

Savannah looked puzzled. "Was it Iris?" she asked.

Margaret shook her head.

"Craig?"

Margaret grinned. "No."

"Damon?"

"No."

"Glenda Cathcart?"

"Noooo."

"Auntie, who? I'm curious."

"Your husband. He stopped by with some medicine we needed for one of the new rescues. Sounds like he's kind of looking forward to doing that project."

"Oh yes, he does enjoy tearing things down and rebuilding. But he doesn't know if he'll be asked to do the job or not. Glenda has to take it before the board. They may want a bonded, bona fide contractor."

Savannah looked down at Lily, smiled, and then glanced toward Lance. "Are you all right?" she asked when she noticed him sitting there, staring down at the cobbler. "You don't have to eat it if you don't like it."

Lance took a breath and relaxed his posture a bit. He gave Savannah a strained smile and said, "No, it's good." He leaned back from the table and said, "I guess I'm just not very hungry." He took a sip of his coffee, set the mug down, and said, his voice cracking, "So your husband's a…" He cleared his throat and started again. "He's a builder? I thought he was a veterinarian."

"That, too," Savannah said grinning. "I call him a weekend renovation warrior."

"Interesting. Ah…when do you think he'll be doing the work at the library?" he asked, his eyes darting from Savannah to Margaret.

Savannah creased her brow. "I don't know. There's no formal work order, yet. Why?"

"Yeah, why?" Margaret said. "Do you want to film the action?"

"Uh, no. Just making small talk." Lance looked at his watch, stood, and said, "Well, I should go. I have a lot to do."

"Well, thanks for coming by to check for damage," Savannah said.

"Huh?" Lance said. "Oh yeah…I'm glad everything's okay."

When Savannah returned after seeing Lance out, she said, "What was that all about?"

"I know exactly what it was about," Margaret said in an angry tone. "He's on the prowl."

"On the prowl?" Savannah questioned.

"Yeah," Margaret said. "For you."

"What?" Savannah shouted.

"You're his next mark—he wants to…"

"He wants to what?" Savannah insisted.

"Well, he wants to conquer you." Margaret said.

"Conquer?"

"Savannah, he's coming on to you. Did he ask if he could see you again…without Michael?"

She thought for a moment and then said, "Well, he did suggest we go somewhere for coffee. He said he doesn't know anyone in town anymore and he'd like to see a friendly face once in a while." She put her face in her hands. "Oh, Auntie, do you really think he wants something more than a friendly face?"

"Yes. I'm absolutely sure of it. He's a player and he wants what he wants. I guess he can usually get it, too. He will push and push."

"What shall I do?" Savannah pleaded.

"Make it perfectly—even rudely—clear that you do not want to have coffee with him or spend any time with him without your husband present. He won't take no for an answer. You will have to be rude. Keep your doors locked. Be wary anytime you go out alone."

"Do you think he would…stalk me?"

"I *know* he would."

"How do you know so much about him?" Savannah asked, point-blank. "You said you dated and it didn't end well. Did he stalk you?"

Margaret sat silent for a moment and then took Savannah's hand. "Vannie, I went out with him a couple of times. We had fun. But I could tell he wasn't that into me. He flirted with every skirt in the room."

"While you were on a date with him?"

"Yes. Well, I met someone at a dance—someone I really liked. I ended it with Lance. When he found out I was dating someone else, he started coming around again. He was relentless. Vannie, you know how upfront and straightforward I can be."

She nodded.

"Well, I was downright rude and he still wouldn't leave me alone. He called. He came to the house whenever Jake would leave. He followed me around. He showed up everywhere I went. It was awful. I finally had to get a restraining order against him. He was not happy—began to threaten me." She thought about it for a minute. "He wants what he can't have and he wants it with a vengeance." She looked her niece in the eye. "Vannie, be careful. Be very careful."

"Do you think he's dangerous?"

"I don't know. I just don't know what he's capable of. But I can tell you it is no fun being stalked—feeling as though you've been violated." She shuddered. "It's an awful way to live."

***

A few days later, Savannah sat on the loveseat in her living room with tears in her eyes as she dialed her phone. "Hi, Craig. This is Savannah."

"Yeah, I know. How are you?"

"Not so good."

"What's wrong, honey?" he asked

"Craig, I'm scared."

"What's happening?"

"Could you come by when you have a chance? I think I'm being stalked."

"What? Who? Listen, I'll be right there."

"Thank you, Craig." She started to end the call and then said into the phone, "Oh Craig, Lily and I are going outside. We'll be on the porch."

Twenty minutes later, Savannah heard Craig drive into their circular driveway. She walked around to the front of the house and met him as he came up the steps.

He frowned when he saw her. "You're shaking." He took her hands, looked into her eyes, and said, "Now tell me, what's going on?"

Savannah pulled away and turned. "Well, I feel kind of silly about calling you, Craig," she said as she led him around to where Lily lay in her swing, "but it has me freaked out." She sat in a cushioned wicker chair, pulled her feet up under her, and motioned for Craig to sit across from her.

Before sitting down, he smiled down at Lily and tickled her tummy. Then he spotted Rags stretched out on the porch. "I see the cat's getting some fresh air."

"Yeah, it's been a while since he's been out. I think he was suffering from cabin fever."

Craig smiled and then looked at Savannah. With concern in his voice, he asked. "So what's going on? Talk to me."

"Well, like I told you on the phone, I think I'm being stalked."

The detective straightened his posture, narrowing his eyes. "What makes you think that?" he asked. "Do you know who it is?"

Savannah bowed her head. "Yes. I know who it is. He keeps calling me. Wants me to have coffee with him. Shows up wherever I go." She raised her voice an octave. "I even saw him in my rearview mirror today when Lily and I were driving back from seeing my horse at my friend Bonnie's stable."

"Who is it?" Craig asked gently.

Savannah took a breath and said, "Lance Grayson."

Craig pressed his lips together in a thin line, slumped a little into the chair, and said, "Well, I'll be…" He focused on Savannah again and lowered is voice. "How long has this been going on?"

She thought for a minute and said, “Three or four days.” She choked up. “Auntie told me he wouldn’t leave me alone—wouldn’t take no for an answer. Boy, was she right.”

“Has he approached you?”

She looked across at him. “Well, yeah. He came here once. My aunt was here, but I don’t think he knew it because she had walked over—her car wasn’t here. Since she was here, I invited him in. He has called me several times since. I don’t answer his calls.”

“Does he leave messages?”

“Yes.” She lowered her head. “He wants to meet for coffee. Just to talk. He’s lonely. Doesn’t know many people here and feels we’re like kindred spirits or something. He’s having some problems in his life and believes that just being with me would help him resolve them. He just wants to be friends, nothing more, he says.”

“And you say he follows you around?”

“Yes, it seems so. Like I said, I saw him on my way back from Bonnie’s today. I run into him at the grocery store. He came into the diner one day when I stopped there to see Iris about something.”

“Savannah, have you told Michael about this?”

She let out a sigh. “No. I don’t want to worry him. And I’m furious about that. We’ve never kept anything from each other.” She pounded her fists on her thighs. “It just makes me so mad that that…man has put me in this position.”

“Savannah, tell your husband what’s going on. Don’t keep this from him. You have to tell him. I’ll bring you a restraining order form and help you go through the process. I don’t want him anywhere near you or anyone else I love.”

Lily began fussing a little and Savannah picked her up, hugging the baby to her. "Do you think he's dangerous?"

Craig avoided eye contact. He cleared his throat.

"Craig?" she said.

"He could be, Savannah. He's on my priority list to get his DNA. I'll do that today." The detective paused and then said quietly, "He has a history of violence. A couple of random incidents at bars, and there are some cases of domestic violence on the books…all with charges dropped."

Savannah took in a ragged breath. "Oh my gosh." She held Lily tightly.

"What time does Michael get home?" Craig asked.

"Could be anytime."

"Okay if I stay until he gets here? I'd like to talk to him." He looked into her eyes. "I want you to talk to him about this, too."

"Okay," she said. She rubbed one of Lily's feet. Kissed her on top of the head.

Craig reached over and tweaked the toes on the baby's other foot. She kicked her foot and smiled.

"Can I get you anything, Craig?" Savannah asked. "Ice water, tea, coffee?"

"Yeah, do you have iced tea or iced coffee? That sounds good."

"I can make some. Want to hold the baby?"

"Sure do," he said. "Come here girlie. Come to Uncle Craig."

Savannah smiled upon hearing Craig begin to recite *Little Miss Muffet Sat on a Tuffet*. She walked over to Craig and kissed him on the cheek.

He looked up at her. "What was that for?"

"Because you're such a good guy," she said, patting him on the shoulder.

Michael walked into the kitchen just as she finished making a glass of iced coffee. "Is that Craig's car in the driveway?" he asked looking around.

"Oh hi, hon. Yes, he's on the porch," she said as she led the way out the side kitchen door. She handed Craig the iced coffee. "Just the way you like it, I hope—cream, two sugars, and lots of ice."

"Ah, looks delicious and refreshing. Thanks."

The two men greeted one another.

"Want an iced coffee, hon?" Savannah asked.

"Sure. Looks good," he said.

This time when she returned to the porch, she noticed that Michael had a strained look on his face. After setting the drink on the small patio table, Michael took Savannah's hand, pulled her gently down on the porch swing next to him, and said quietly, "Savannah, Craig says someone's been bothering you. What's this all about? Why didn't you tell me?"

"Oh Michael," she said, tears spilling over onto her cheeks, "I thought I could take care of it without bothering you. I'm so sorry. Craig's right. I should have told you when it started." She shook her head. "I didn't know he would keep pursuing me." She began to sob. "I did everything to discourage him."

"Awww, honey," he said as he wrapped his arms around her and held her close. "It's okay. I'm not mad at you. But I am worried. Of course, I'm worried and angry. Who is this guy? Do you know him? Is it someone we know?"

Savannah nodded. "Yeah, we know him. It's Lance Grayson."

Michael pinched his lips together. He looked as if he would explode. He took in a deep breath and gritted his teeth. "The nerve of that jerk," he hissed. "Who does he think he is, trying to get in the middle of our life like that?" He looked at Craig. "So what can you do about it? Can you arrest him?"

Craig shook his head. "I'm afraid not, Michael…at least not at this point." He handed Lily the stuffed kitty she had dropped for the umpteenth time and said, "But, as I told Savannah, I need to do a DNA test on him in the murder case."

Michael lurched forward and looked Craig sternly in the face. "You think he's the killer? A murderer is after my wife? That is *not* acceptable, Craig. You have to do something!"

Craig put up his hand. "No, he hasn't been accused. There's no evidence indicating that he killed Julie. Cheryl is still on our radar. But we have to cover all our bases. Someone was sleeping with that woman before she was killed and I aim to find out who it was."

Craig tickled Lily's tummy and laughed when she gurgled at him. "Well, as much as I hate to leave the company of such a lovely young lady, Uncle Craig has to go."

Lily began to fuss and he said, "I know I'm your favorite uncle. I'll come back and play with you another day, okay? Now go drool on your daddy for a while," he said as he handed the baby over to Michael.

"Wait, where's Rags?" Savannah shouted. She quickly stood and began to look around. "Craig, did you see him take off?" she asked.

He shook his head and joined her in the search. As the duo reached the far south side of the large porch, he said, "There he is. Over by those big bushes."

"Rags," Savannah called. "Where do you think you're going?"

Michael caught up with the pair, pointed, and said, "Looks like he's fixing to climb that tree." He chuckled. "Oops, there he goes."

Savannah jogged toward the cat and attempted to grab him before he was out of her reach. "Dang," she said, "I knew I couldn't trust him." She pushed her side bangs off her forehead and said, "He was just lying there so nicely, so I took the leash off. Then I turned my back."

"And Rags took advantage," Michael said.

Craig stood back, an amused grin on his face as he watched Savannah attempt to lure the cat down out of the bushy tree.

"Here," Michael said, handing Lily to the detective. He walked over to where Savannah stood and looked up at the cat, who was all but hidden by the thick foliage. "Rags, come down from there, will you?"

"Maybe he'll go in the house if we open that upstairs window," Savannah suggested. "I haven't ordered a new screen since the other one was damaged when Julie…"

"I just hope he doesn't hang himself with that harness," he said. "Savannah, why did you take the leash off? You know you can't trust him." He didn't notice his wife stifling tears. He was too intent on getting his hands on the cat. "Where's the ladder?" he asked.

Savannah took in a ragged breath and said, "I'll get it."

"No, just tell me where it is," he said. "It's heavy."

"Out by the corral, I think—behind the tack room."

"I'll be right back," he said. "Keep an eye on the cat, will ya?"

Savannah nodded, still near tears. She glanced at Craig, who was staring up toward the cat. "Savannah," he said, walking closer to the thick, brushy tree, "is that something stuck up there in the tree?" He peered up into the limbs. "What is that?"

"What?" she asked, moving toward him.

"That red thing just above the cat, there."

"I don't' know," she said.

"Do you see it?"

"Yes, I can see a little bit of red. I can't tell what it is, though. Rags seems to be interested in it."

"Okay, move back," Michael ordered when he returned with the ladder.

"Michael," Savannah said, "there's something in the tree. See if you can tell what it is."

"I'm not on a treasure hunt, Savannah. I just want to get the cat out of there before he hurts himself."

Savannah and Craig looked at one another and rolled their eyes. "Testy, isn't he?" she whispered.

"He's under a lot of pressure right now," Craig explained.

Savannah lowered her eyes. "Yeah, I know."

"Well, I'll be," Michael said.

"What?" Savannah asked eagerly.

"It's Adam's fire engine."

Savannah scrunched up her face. "In the tree? Well, that's odd. Can you get it?"

"Maybe," he said.

"Wait!" Craig shouted.

Both Savannah and Michael looked in the detective's direction.

"It could be a clue," Craig explained. "We need to treat it as evidence. Let me get it so we don't compromise any prints."

"What?" Michael said. "Evidence? Heck, Craig, Adam probably knocked it off the window sill without knowing it or tossed it out the window for some reason. It's just a toy."

"That's not right," Savannah said. "There's always a screen on that window. He would never take the screen off and toss his fire engine out."

Michael scratched his head. "Well, okay then. Let me get the cat down and you can go up and get the…evidence," he said. "Come on Rags. Looks like you've uncovered another clue."

A few minutes later, Craig lowered himself down the ladder, Adam's fire engine under one arm wrapped in a towel Savannah had given him. He looked down at Rags, who was now attached to a leash and under Michael's control. "So, your cat has done it again…or so it seems," he said. "It'll be interesting to see what secrets this toy holds, if any." He looked up into the tree and said, "Right under our noses—we just couldn't see it for the thick branches."

"So what can you do to offer protection for my wife?" Michael asked as he walked with Craig toward his car.

"I'll have a talk with Grayson and we'll start the process to prepare a restraining order."

"What good does a restraining order do?" Michael asked.

"If Savannah sees him anywhere near where she is, she can call the police and have him arrested." Craig leaned toward Michael. "Technically, there will be a distance written into the document—100 yards or something. But I figure if Savannah can see him and he's not walking away from her, he's violating the order."

Michael scowled. "I'd like to violate his space with my fist," he said.

"Take it easy, Michael," Craig said. "I'm pretty sure I can take care of this for you."

Michael watched the detective drive out the driveway and then he joined Savannah at the front door. He wrapped both arms around her and held her in a bear hug for a few minutes before saying, "I'm sorry I snapped at you. It's just that…" his voice cracked.

"I know hon." She kissed him. "What do you say we have some dinner?"

After the couple shared a chicken Caesar salad, Savannah filled the dishwasher and then went looking for Michael and Lily. "There you two are," she said, when she stepped into the nursery and saw Michael rocking the baby. Rags stood on Lily's dresser staring down at them and Buffy was curled up at Michael's feet. Savannah put her finger up to her lips and whispered, "Shhhh. She's asleep."

Before Michael laid Lily gently in the crib, Savannah kissed her and picked up the baby monitor. "Night-night, Buffy," she said as the couple walked out of the room. "Rags, you come with us." She watched as he leaped from the dresser and chased down the hallway into the living room.

"You're brooding," Savannah said once they were settled on the loveseat.

"Am I?" he asked.

"I hate it when you brood."

"I hate it when you keep something important from me."

She took in a ragged breath. "I know, honey. I'm so sorry."

Michael squeezed Savannah's hand. "It's okay." She turned around so she was facing him and laid her head on his chest. He wrapped both arms around her and cradled her. No words were spoken until he said into her hair, "Savannah, he didn't…try to…touch you, did he?"

She pulled away. "No!" she almost shouted. "If he had, I would have…"

Michael looked at her as if he was amused. "You would have what?" he asked with a sideways smile.

"I would have hit him where it hurts and…"

He took on a more serious demeanor. "Savannah, maybe you should carry pepper spray." He straightened his posture. "You know, they teach that self-defense class at the recreation center. Seriously, I'd like to see you take that."

"What, you want a jock for a wife?"

He shook his head. "No, what I want is to be with you and Lily every minute of every day so I'm sure that you're always safe. That's what I want," he said holding her hard against him.

The silence that followed was interrupted when Michael's cell phone rang. He pulled it out of his pocket. "It's Glenda Cathcart," he said.

After ending the call, he said, his voice full of excitement, "Well, it looks as if Damon and I have a job."

"Oh, you're going to unveil that secret room? What do you think you'll find?"

"Probably dirt, grime, and black widows. I'm glad we're not on the cleaning committee. That's going to be a job."

"When will you start?" Savannah asked.

"Not sure. There are things to work out before the contract is issued."

***

The following day, Michael used his key to unlock the front door of the house. "I'm home," he called out.

"In here," Savannah shouted.

"Where?" he asked.

"Kitchen," she said as she peered at him from the doorway, stirring spoon in hand. "I'm making a new mac and cheese recipe with crab and I'm at the stirring stage," she said as he entered.

He walked up behind her at the stove and kissed her on the neck. "Everything okay today?" he asked into her ear.

"Yeah," she said as if relieved. "Everything today is good. Lily and I didn't even leave the house. Had a lazy day at home." She turned toward him. "I really enjoyed it." Looking at their baby in the cradle swing, she said, "I think she did, too."

Michael walked over and picked up Lily, sat down with her, and began talking to her about her day at home with Mommy and the animals.

"Tell us about *your* day," Savannah prompted.

"Well," he said to Lily in a sing-song fashion, "a big brown dog with a hurt leg visited Daddy this morning. I had to put a biiiiig cast on his leg. A little while later," he said with animation, "I got to go outside and give a big horsey a shot. Then," he said with flair, "a couple of baaaaby kitties came to see me. I weighed them, I petted them, I looked in their mouths…"

By then Savannah was laughing out loud at his attempt to make the mundane story appealing to their daughter and the fact that Lily was absolutely mesmerized. "She is really into your story, there. Maybe she *will* be a veterinarian."

Michael continued telling the story to the baby and then looked up at Savannah, "Hey, where's the paper? I heard there was a story in there about the secret room at the library."

"Oh yes, there's an old picture taken in that room when it was open and a story about how the board has hired contractors to restore it for library use."

"Contractors, huh?"

"Yeah, how are they getting around using a licensed contractor, Michael? My aunt was asking me that today."

"It's not that big of a job, actually. And someone on the board has arranged for us to work under his license. It's all on the up-and-up for a small town, you know."

"So you're starting this weekend?"

"Was that in the story, too? Yeah, I talked to Damon and I think we're going to start the demolition Sunday. They want us to work after hours and on Sunday, which works out well for us." Michael became quiet for a moment. Finally, he asked, "Savannah, he didn't come around today did he?"

She stopped stirring the pot and looked over at her husband. She shook her head. "No. Not that I know of. No phone calls…nothing. Thank heavens!" She set the spoon down, wiped her hands on a nearby towel, and said, "Oh, that reminds me. Craig's coming over this evening. Says he has something he wants to tell us. Also, he'll bring the restraining order for me to sign." She looked at the clock. "He should be here in an hour."

Chapter 7

When Craig arrived, his demeanor seemed dour.

Michael was first to greet him. "Uh-oh, doesn't look like you're bringing good news."

"Not really," Craig said. "…just not much news. It's been a long day."

"Come on in," Michael invited.

Before the men could sit down, Savannah appeared with the baby monitor in her hand. Craig looked up. "Oh, did I miss seeing the angel girl?" he asked, sounding disappointed. "She was going to be my only bright spot today."

"Well, come on, then," Savannah said. "She's sleeping, but you can peek in on her if you like."

The rugged detective gazed down at the sleeping baby through blue eyes under graying brows. Savannah heard him sigh. He smoothed Lily's soft hair with one hand and said, "This is what it's all about, isn't it, guys?"

Savannah and Michael nodded. Savannah kissed her hand and softly patted the baby's chubby cheek with it. "Night-night," she said just before they exited the nursery.

"Thank you," Craig said when they'd settled in the living room. "That's the reality fix I needed."

"Reality fix?" Savannah questioned.

"Yeah, like I said, this is what it's all about—our precious, innocent little ones. So important." He looked at Michael and then at Savannah. "They are our future, you know. And we have to prepare them." He looked down at the folder he held in his hands. "If we don't prepare them, they may not make it in the world outside of their innocence."

Craig suddenly looked up. "Sorry guys. I got lost in my thoughts there for a minute. Just thinking about all of the kids who don't get the love, care, and guidance they're entitled to and those who get it and still mess up."

Savannah softened her voice. "You're thinking about your son, aren't you, Craig?"

He took a deep breath and sat up straighter. "Yes, and all of the what-ifs that drive the parent of a dead child crazy."

"How long ago did you lose him?" she asked.

"Oh gosh, it's been nearly twenty years." He ran his hand over his chin and said, "But I've been given somewhat of a second chance, getting to be involved with Iris's boys." He looked from Michael to Savannah. "You know, Damon and I have become great friends."

"That is so awesome," Michael said. "He's a super young man." He pointed at Craig. "You know, he and I have a construction project."

Craig smiled. "Yeah, I heard about that. He's looking forward to 'learning from the master,' as he says."

Michael looked down, shaking his head. "I don't know about that. But I'm looking forward to the project, too."

"Good," Craig said. He then slapped the file folder on his lap. "Now, for the reason I wanted to see you two…I have the restraining order form here. Savannah, all you have to do is sign it, take it to the clerk, and appear in court. You haven't seen that jerk around you since we talked, have you?"

"No, thank heavens," Savannah said. "I presumed you had a talk with him."

"Yeah. That I did. That I did," Craig said, narrowing his eyes. "He'd be a fool to bother you again."

Savannah's eyes widened. "Oh gosh. What did you do to him?"

Craig just looked at her with a sideways grin.

"Whatever it was, thank you, Craig," Michael said, taking Savannah's hand and squeezing it.

"You are welcome." He smirked, saying, "It was a pleasure."

"Now what about the investigation, Craig?" Savannah asked.

"Well, we've been questioning Cheryl. She doesn't know how her scarf ended up in Julie's room. I'm inclined to believe her, although her DNA was on the body, as was Lance's."

"So they attacked her together?" Savannah asked, her eyes wide.

Craig chuckled. "I hadn't thought of that. Maybe. But no, I'm thinking it was because Julie and Cheryl had that scuffle earlier in the day. And we all saw Lance all over her that afternoon, too."

Savannah rolled her eyes. "We sure did."

Craig looked thoughtful for a moment. "I have a question. Do either of you remember Cheryl or Lance handling Adam's fire engine at any time? Did either of them have access to it that you know of?"

Michael frowned. "Why?"

Craig mumbled, "Murder weapon."

"What?" Savannah and Michael asked.

Craig took a deep breath. "It was the murder weapon, guys."

"Good lord," Michael said, dropping his head. "I was hoping that wasn't the case."

"It was one of his special toys," Savannah said.

"We'll get it back to you eventually."

"No!" Savannah almost shouted. "We'll get him another one. We don't want that back."

"I agree," Michael said with a scowl.

"So whose prints did you find on it?" Savannah asked.

"Both," Craig said.

"Both Lance and Cheryl?" Michael asked.

He nodded. "You got it. So did you see either of them handling that toy?"

Michael and Savannah looked at one another and then back at Craig. "Heck, I don't think so," Savannah said.

"Well, tell me this—were either of them in that room at any time that you know of?"

Savannah leaned forward. "Yeah, both of them. Everyone walked up the stairs with us that morning when we were assigning rooms."

Michael chuckled. "Assigning rooms? You sound like some sort of cruise director."

Savannah slapped at him playfully. "Oh stop. You know what I mean. I showed Adam's room second—after showing DeeDee and Raymond the healing room…er…uh, the room at the top of the stairs on the left."

Craig expressed keen interest. "So everyone went into Adam's room that morning…with the exception of DeeDee and her husband?"

Savannah thought for a moment. "Well, yeah, I guess so." She then leaned forward and said, "Actually, DeeDee and Raymond also came into Adam's room. But not Crank and James. They didn't come in at all." Craig looked confused. "Well, everyone wanted to see all the rooms." She paused and then looked point-blank at Craig and said, "That's when I remembered that Cheryl and Julie would probably not want to bunk together and I offered the option of the nursery to one of them."

"So Cheryl and Lance were both inside the room where Julie slept that night, is that right?" Craig asked.

Savannah nodded. "Yes."

He looked into her face. "Did you see either of them touch that toy fire engine?"

"Let's see, someone picked it up. That I remember. I mean, it's really an interesting toy, don't you think? And Adam keeps it on that shelf just inside the door. It would be easy for someone just barely stepping into that room to see it and want to touch it."

"Show me, would you?"

"Show you where the fire engine was?"

"Yes."

Once inside Adam's room, Savannah pointed to the shelf where the fire engine always sat. She then gasped. "I do remember something," she said. "Rob picked the fire engine up. I saw him out the corner of my eye. He held it toward Lance and said something like, 'did you ever have any toys as sophisticated as this?' Lance took it and…"

"Lance held it in his hands, then?" Craig asked for clarification.

"Yes," she said, her memory of that incident now clear. "Lance examined it, handed it back to Rob, and Rob held it over to Cheryl and teased her with it."

"Teased her?" Craig said.

"Yes, he held it up close to her and made siren sounds." She sighed. "Filmmakers can be so juvenile. They were always doing things like that—like a bunch of kids."

"So what did Cheryl do?" Craig asked.

"She put her hands up and pushed the engine away from her face."

"So she put her hands on the toy, is that right?"

"Yes, she did, as a matter of fact," Savannah said. "Both Cheryl and Lance touched it and so did Rob."

"Damn!" Craig said. "There goes my open-and-shut case."

***

The following Sunday morning, Michael and Damon headed for the library. "Are you ready to learn the building business?" Michael asked.

"Yeah. Sure am."

"You won't give up your day job, will you?"

"Naw." Damon hesitated and then said, "I might leave the newspaper at some point, but I don't plan to give up writing. I'm hooked." He chuckled. "Colbi says I found my passion in prison." He thought for a moment and then said, "You wouldn't be able to give up your veterinary practice, would you?"

"No. Nor would I be happy if I couldn't work with wood." Michael glanced at his passenger and said, "Passion, huh? I guess helping animals, educating people about animals, and working with wood are my passions."

Upon arriving at the library, the two men used the key Glenda had given them to enter through the heavy gate into the secret garden. Michael looked around. "Here we are. Nobody around. Not too hot. Good working conditions. Shall we get started?"

"Sure, you take the lead. I'll follow," Damon said. "So where do we start?"

"Here," Michael said, handing Damon a large sledge hammer. "Demolition."

Once the men had taken down the wall and part of the deck on the other side of it, they walked down all eleven steps into a dark and dank room. As they looked around with flashlights, Michael remarked, "I still can't believe they didn't clean out this room before building that wall. Must have been a quickie job."

Damon removed his baseball cap and slid it back on again. "Hey, there's the little light we saw through the hole," he said. "Look, it's a chest freezer…still plugged in."

The two men looked askance at their discovery. "That's really strange, isn't it? I mean, why would a library need a freezer—especially one that size. Must be fifteen cubic feet. It would hold a lot."

"If they had a microwave, I'd say it was for their frozen weight-loss lunches or something," Damon said. "But why would they leave it down here like that?"

"Well, shall we see what's for dinner?" Michael quipped as he prepared to lift the lid. "Locked," he said, when the lid refused to budge.

"Or frozen shut," Damon suggested.

"Do you see a key hanging anywhere?"

"No," he said shining his light around, "but I see a nail right there above the freezer where one might have hung. Maybe a rat knocked it off." Damon knelt down and searched the floor with his flashlight. Finding nothing, he said, as if thinking out loud, "This sure is a strange place for a freezer. I wonder how long it's been running."

Michael shined his flashlight over and around the freezer. "Probably for as long as this room has been boarded up—maybe four years or more." He stared at the dust-covered unit. "Maybe a hunter stored his venison inside and brought it over here so he didn't have to pay the electric bill."

"But how would he get to his meat when he got hungry?" Damon asked, playing devil's advocate.

"Okay," Michael said, "maybe the guy died or moved away and forgot about it." He stared down at the freezer. "You know, I'm sure they're just going to toss this old thing out anyway. Is there any reason why we can't break into it? I'd like to find out what's in it before we commit it to the dump."

"So what do you think we need—a crowbar?" Damon asked.

"Yeah." Michael looked at his watch. He said, "I have an appointment with a sick rescue dog over at Zelma's place soon. Won't take long. How about we spend this morning taking measurements and making a list of what we'll need. You can go with me on the call and then we'll get our supplies. We'll bring a crowbar back with us."

"So tell me what you propose we do," Damon said. "I can't quite visualize how we'll get from point A to point B."

Michael took off his cap and scratched his head. "Well, I could tell you what I envision, but it might be easier for both of us if we just start working and we can talk about it as we go. What I think will work now, might not work when we get to that point. But our objective is to extend the walls on the sides of the staircase, out and around it." He climbed the stairs and motioned. "…out to here. Then we'll install a sturdy door with a good lock. Can you visualize it?"

"Yeah, I can. I'm just not sure how the construction will go." He looked around and asked, "What about the deck?"

Michael surveyed the situation beyond the stairwell and said, "There's no reason why we can't build a new wall beyond the stairwell opening and preserve the deck. What do you think?" When Damon looked confused, Michael said, "Once you've done a few jobs like this, you'll get the knack for visualizing the process. It takes practice."

***

Two hours later, after treating the injured dog, ordering materials at Michael's favorite building supply company, and grabbing a quick lunch, the pair returned to the library.

"When will they deliver the rest of the stuff?" Damon asked.

"Hopefully, this afternoon. If not, I'll meet them here tomorrow after hours. I want to rig some lights in case we feel like working into the night."

"Sounds good," Damon said. "So how long do you think this job will take?"

"Probably most of the week, working nights. We may need next Sunday to finish. We'll see how it goes." Michael looked over at Damon. "Are ya ready, guy?" he asked.

"Sure."

The men struggled to carry in the supplies they'd purchased. Once inside the secret garden, Michael said, "This is not an ideal set-up, but it's nice to have all this space just outside the room. We can set up downstairs for the work down there and up here for the work at this level. Kinda convenient." He turned to Damon. "Not every job is convenient. Sometimes you have to get in some pretty contorted positions."

"Will we have to break down every night?"

"No. I promised to finish in a week if they will keep this area closed off for the duration. No secret garden for the next week," Michael said. "And the staff and volunteer deck will be off-limits, too, until we get a new wall up. Thankfully, there is a solid wall surrounding three sides of the deck, so it is secure, as long as they keep the doors locked from the library proper to the courtyard and the deck until we've finished building."

Yes, that will be convenient," Damon said. "Where do you want these?" he asked, holding up a couple of Michael's tools.

"Downstairs, if you don't mind," he said.

A few minutes later, Michael heard Damon call out, "Michael! Michael! Come down here! You're not going to believe this!"

"What? Did you find a big rat?" he said laughing.

"No! Hurry!" Damon said.

Michael rushed down the steps to find Damon shining his flashlight toward a bare wall where the freezer had been just hours earlier. "What the heck…" Michael said under his breath. Suddenly he turned and scanned the area with his own flashlight and let out a sigh of relief. "All my tools seem to be here."

"But why would anyone come in here and take that old freezer?" Damon asked.

"Man, I don't know," Michael said. "This just keeps getting weirder."

Chapter 8

Michael pulled into his driveway just after dark Sunday evening and parked. "Oh, hi, hon," he said as he stepped up onto the wrap-around porch and saw Savannah standing in the doorway.

"Gosh, you look beat, Michael," she said as they entered the living room. How'd the project at the library go? Did you enjoy mentoring Damon?"

Michael eased out of his jacket and removed his baseball cap, tossing both on the loveseat. "It went pretty well," he said, as he sat and pulled off his shoes and socks. He leaned back and said, "Yeah, we got a lot done and had a good time. Damon's a pretty good worker and a fast learner."

"So what did you find in that secret room once you tore the wall down? Anything creepy?" she asked.

He laughed. "Creepy? Yeah, there were creepy crawlers, for sure." He ran his hand through his hair. "The games and puzzles Maggie talked about were still there. Can you believe it?"

"You mean that room was frozen in time and space?" Savannah said. "Now that's eerie, don't you think?"

He sat up, his eyes wide. "You want to hear something eerie? Damon and I still can't believe it."

"What?" she asked.

"There was this old freezer down there; plugged in and running."

"Really?" she said. "Now that is weird."

"But wait until you hear this. So we leave for a couple of hours to buy supplies and grab a bite to eat. When we get back, that freezer is gone."

Savannah creased her brow. "What? Gone? But who would…?"

"I don't have a clue." He hesitated and then said, "Someone with a key, I guess. We locked everything up. I left my tools…"

"Did they take your tools?"

"No. Not even that new drill I just bought. Just the old freezer."

"What was in it, do you know?" she asked.

"Don't know. It was locked. We brought back a crowbar to pry it open before we disposed of it. But it was already gone." He shook his head. "A real mystery."

"Did you tell Craig?"

"Craig?" Michael looked puzzled. "Why?"

"Well, it was a burglary, for one thing, and for another, it's just plain bizarre. It might be connected to other burglaries or something." She jumped a little in excitement. "Hey, you know how people sometimes hide their valuables in their home freezers? Maybe there's a burglary ring stealing freezers and fridges for the valuables."

Michael just stared at Savannah as she continued. "Or maybe they're stealing appliances for the metal. Is there copper or some other sought-after metal in old freezers? Or maybe it's an antique."

Michael shook his head and grinned. "Savannah, sometimes I think Craig's right—you would make a good detective. You sure have an imagination for it." He thought for a moment and then said, "Maybe you're right…"

"About old freezers being valuable?"

"Noooo, about calling Craig. I might as well let him know. I already texted Glenda and told her. She was as surprised as we were to learn that there was a freezer down there. She knew nothing about it. She's going to ask around to see if anyone else knew about it."

"Where are you?" Michael said, after finishing his call to Craig.

"Kitchen," Savannah responded. "So what did he say?" she asked when she saw him walk in.

"He said as far as he knows this was the first case of a missing freezer ever reported in this county." He laughed. "I don't think finding it is very high on his priority list." He looked over Savannah's shoulder as she stood at the kitchen counter. "What's for dinner?"

"Spaghetti and turkey meatballs and a spinach salad."

"Mmmm. My favorite."

"Oh, you say that every night. I could serve you jelly-bean stew or chicken-liver sandwiches and you'd say, 'Mmmm, my favorite.'"

"And there's something wrong with that?" he asked.

"No," she said winking at him. "I love that you're so agreeable."

"Hey, I figure if I complain, I'll find myself wearing the apron."

"You got that right. Now sit down and let's eat."

Michael was nearly finished with his meal when he set his fork down and said, "Oh, I forgot to tell you. Craig said he talked at length with Cheryl and he thinks he knows why she and Julie hated each other so much."

"Why?" Savannah asked.

"Lance Grayson."

"Huh?"

"I guess Cheryl and Lance were a couple—or so Cheryl thought. But Cheryl found out that he was also seeing Julie, who evidently thought *she* was Lance's one-and-only." He shook his head in disgust. "That guy seems to cause a lot of damage wherever he goes—at least where women are concerned." He cut into a meatball and started to take a bite.

Savannah was quiet for a moment and then she said, "Michael…he called me today."

Michael dropped his fork onto his plate. "What?"

"I didn't answer. He didn't leave a message. It could be that he dialed my number by mistake."

"So you're still willing to give that jerk the benefit of the doubt, are you? Well, I'm not. As far as I'm concerned, he has broken the restraining order. I'm going to have him arrested." Michael reached for his phone. He looked at it and said more calmly, "I have a call." He eyed the screen and said, "I don't know this number." He hesitated and then decided to answer it.

"Hello? What? Who is this? Go to hell!"

Savannah stared over at her husband with fear in her eyes. "Michael, who was that? What did they say?"

He didn't respond. Instead he dialed a number on his phone. "Craig, it's Michael again. Listen, I just got a threatening call. No. I don't know who it was. The voice was weird—like disguised. He seemed to think that I know something and I don't know what that would be. He said that if I talk about what I found, he would hurt me. He said, 'I'll hurt you bad.' Damn Craig, what's going on? Do you know? I haven't found anything that should incriminate anyone." Michael stood, ran his hand through his hair, and began pacing. "Or maybe I have and I just don't know what it is. What do you think this is all about, Craig?"

Michael listened for a moment and then said, "What have I been doing lately? Well, my regular work with my regular patients. Oh, I did go out to a ranch last week owned by a new couple from Frisco. I started the library project today, as you know. That's it…absolutely nothing out of the ordinary." He took in a short breath and said, "Hey, could it have something to do with us finding Adam's fire engine?"

After another moment, he said, "Okay, Craig. I'll do that. Thanks."

When Michael finished the call, he turned toward Savannah, who sat with her hands over her mouth and tears welling up in her eyes. He knelt next to her and took her hand. Speaking more quietly now, he said, "Craig told me just to be wary. It could be a prank call or the wrong number. Or… someone thinks I know something about Julie's murder, which is ridiculous."

***

"Is everything alright, Michael?" Damon asked as the two of them drove to the library the following evening after work.

"Yeah," he said. "Just a little…tired. That's all."

"Had a busy day at work, huh?"

"Yeah." He glanced over at Damon as he drove. "Only not too tired to show you a thing or two about building," he said, punching Damon in the shoulder playfully.

Damon grinned. "Okay, then."

The men had been working at the lower level for an hour under the lights they had rigged when suddenly everything went dark. "What the…?" Michael said. "Must have blown the circuit. Where did we leave those flashlights?"

Just then Michael realized they weren't alone; someone else had joined them. Even in the nearly dark room, he could see a glint of light reflecting from something in the intruder's hand. *A gun,* he thought. He looked into the stranger's face. It was black. As the figure moved closer, Michael could see that he (or she) was wearing a ski mask, eyes shining through the cut-outs in the dim light.

"I'm sorry you found it, Michael. I really am. It's a shame your little girl will grow up without a daddy. And that great-looking wife of yours. She'll miss you for a while, but it won't take her long to find someone else."

"Who the hell are you?" Michael demanded. "What do you want?"

"It's too late. You know too much," the distorted voice said. "I can't let you take me down—not in my prime—not for something that wasn't my fault."

I have to act fast, Michael thought. *I can't let this maniac kill me.* He glanced up at Damon, who was standing in the shadows observing the scene, seemingly unnoticed by the gunman. *Maybe Damon can slip out behind this guy and call for help. I'll see if I can distract him so Damon can escape.* "Hey, I have no intentions of taking you down," he said. "I know it wasn't your fault. In fact, I can help you if you'll just tell me what you're afraid of."

The gunman laughed. "Afraid? You're the one who should be afraid. You're minutes—maybe seconds—away from being dead," the gravelly voice said.

"Well, don't let me die without knowing why. Give me that, would you?"

The intruder stood silent. He took his eyes off Michael for a moment and glanced around him. Suddenly he walked a few steps to the right, knelt down and picked something up. "I want to be sure I hit the mark," he said, shining a flashlight toward Michael.

Michael closed his eyes momentarily and thought about his family and their beautiful life. *Where is Damon, dammit?* he thought. *Wait, is that a siren? It's close. Are they coming here?*

When he opened his eyes, the gunman was gone. So was Damon. He stood alone in the dank room, which was dimly lit by the fading light of dusk. *What now?* He wondered. *God, where is Damon? What is that jerk doing up there? Is it safe to go up?* "Damon," he whispered loudly. There was no answer. *I've gotta take a chance,* he thought, as he rushed up the steps to the secret garden. He stopped as he approached the landing and noticed that the door into the library was standing wide open. *I'm not going in there,* he thought. *Too many places to hide. If the cops are here, the gunman might be hiding in there. But where's Damon? God, let him be okay.*

Just then, Michael heard a hushed voice from across the patio. "In here, Ben."

"Damon, is that you?" Michael whispered loudly.

"Yeah. Deputy Ben's with me."

Michael looked toward the voice and saw Deputy Ben walking cautiously through the gate on the north side of the secret garden, gun drawn. "He may be hiding in there," Michael whispered, pointing to the open door. He stood back as the deputy eased his way through the door into the library.

"Let's go back down there, Damon—come on—out of the line of any fire," Michael said, quickly leading Damon down the steps to safety. They crouched out of sight and listened. It seemed like forever before they heard anything coming from the library.

"Stop or I'll shoot! Stop!"

Bang! Bang!

"Holy sh…" Damon said.

They heard scuffling above them, another shot, and then silence. Within a few moments, they heard voices. "Hey, where are you guys?" one shouted.

"Down here," Michael said. "Can we come out?"

"Yeah, he got away, dammit."

"Did you shoot him?" Damon asked.

"No."

Once Michael and Damon emerged from the sunken room, they saw Deputies Jim and Ben standing just outside the library door. Jim said, "He waited until Ben and I were both on the south side of the library and he scooted out the front door. We shot into the air, but he didn't return fire, nor did he stop. Just ran like hell. I have another unit on his tail. But in this neighborhood, once he takes that ski mask off, he'll just blend in and go unnoticed. Do you know who it is?" he asked.

Both Michael and Damon shook their heads. "Not a clue," Michael said. "But he wants me dead for some reason." He swallowed hard. "I think he would have gotten his wish if you guys hadn't shown up so fast. How did you know about this, anyway?"

"Damon called us."

"That quickly—and without the gunman knowing?" he asked.

"Well, we were in the vicinity. We were on another call when this one came in. We split off from the medical call down the street, doubled back, and came here."

"So the sirens weren't for this call?"

"No, we were just driving by, sirens on—guess that's what made the gunman run, huh?"

Michael shook his head in disbelief. "A coincidence that may have saved our lives."

Just then, they heard another voice. "Hey, when did they put this gate in here?"

Damon called out in recognition, "Craig!"

Deputy Jim nodded. "Detective," he said in greeting.

"How'd you…?" Damon started.

Craig grinned. "Damon, you know you can't keep anything from me. If you're in trouble, I'm gonna to find out about it." He took on a more serious demeanor. "Everything okay here?" he asked.

"Yeah, now it is," Damon said. "But the guy got away."

"What happened?" Craig asked.

"Well, this guy just sneaked in here and threatened to kill me because of what I know—which is nothing," Michael said.

"Damn, does it ever end?" Craig said, picking up his vibrating cell phone. "Yeah, Sledge here," he practically shouted into the phone.

Michael and Damon continued to answer Jim's questions. "Do you have a key to the main part of the library?" he asked.

Michael shook his head. "No, just this courtyard patio gate."

"How do you suppose the library got open?" he asked.

"Heck if I know. I just assumed it was locked. Maybe it wasn't," Michael said.

"Or maybe that guy has a key," Damon offered. "He might work here or something."

"Hmmm, I'll check with the librarian about who has keys to this door."

When Craig ended his call, he approached the men and said, "Excuse me, but I need to go check something out. They've found a body in Walston Canyon." He shook his head, muttering, "No rest for the weary."

Before exiting through the gate, he turned and said, "Michael and Damon, I suggest you quit for the day and stop the project until we get a bead on this guy."

The two men nodded.

Craig started to step out, but stopped again. "Do you know when they put this gate in here?"

Damon shook his head. "It's probably been there forever. It was just hidden behind those bushes." He grinned. "It is a secret garden, after all."

Craig glanced around the area for a moment and then promptly left.

***

Later that evening, Michael's phone rang. "Michael, it's Craig."

"Hi Craig, what's up?"

"Well, I have a few questions for you."

"More questions?" he said, feigning annoyance. "Sure, shoot."

"I also have something to show you. Can I come by?"

Michael glanced at Savannah, who was reading from her Kindle. "Sure, we're just hanging out. Come on over."

Savannah looked up as he ended the call. "Craig's coming over?"

"Yes, says he has something to show me, and more questions."

Savannah turned off the e-reader and leaned forward in the overstuffed chair. "Michael, I am so freaked out about what happened to you today. You're not going back to work at the library until that creep is caught, are you?"

"No. I wouldn't put Damon or myself in that kind of danger. No way."

Fifteen minutes later, Michael ushered Craig in and they sat down across from Savannah. "How are you two this evening? Everything good?" Craig asked.

"Uh, yeah. Pretty good," Savannah said. "How're things with you? Looks like you're working late."

"Gotta put in the hours if you wanna catch the bad guys," he said.

"So have you caught any bad guys today?" Michael asked.

"'Fraid not. But we're on a trail." When there was no verbal response, Craig continued. "Michael, tell me about the freezer you saw at the library, will you?"

Startled, Michael said, "Oh…uh, it was a chest freezer, I'd say about five-by-four-by-maybe-four. It was white—very dirty."

"Did you look inside?"

"No, it was locked. We left to get a crowbar to open it, figured we'd find it full of venison. When we returned, the freezer was gone."

"Do you know what brand it was?"

Michael shook his head slowly. "No, I didn't notice that. Maybe Damon did." He started to take a sip from his water bottle, then said, "I can tell you it has a small red light that shows when the thing is plugged in and running."

"Is this it?" Craig asked showing Michael a photograph.

"Yeah, looks like the same one." He looked at Craig inquisitively. "Why are you interested in the freezer?"

Craig cleared his throat. "Well, we think we found it."

Michael frowned. "Where?"

"Deep in a canyon where it would have been hidden…maybe forever…except for a dog."

"A dog?" Savannah asked.

"Yes, a group of hikers lost their dog. He went after a rabbit or something and got himself in trouble—slid down into this canyon. One of the hikers went down after him and he became stuck. When the rescue folks got there, one of them saw this freezer lying sideways in the brush, the lid open and the contents lying out in front of it." He looked at Savannah and then Michael. "The contents wasn't venison, but you were close. It was a body."

"What?" Michael said. He stood and began pacing. He stopped and turned toward Craig. "Who was it?" he asked.

"We're working on a positive, but we think we've found a missing person who's been gone for about four years. No ID yet."

Michael ran his hand through his hair. "Good lord," he said.

"And he's been in that freezer in the library all this time?" Savannah asked.

"Looks that way," Craig said.

"So the guy who's been threatening me must have put him there, right?"

"Yeah, I'm pretty sure of that. But we don't know who it is, yet. We should get the results back this evening. If the victim is who I think it is, Savannah, I'd like to engage your assistance with something."

"Me? To do what?" she asked.

"Well, if this is Chris Sparks, I need to speak with his wife and, from what I understand, she won't let a man near her. Have either of you ever met Leslie Sparks?"

Michael and Savannah both shook their heads.

"From the pictures I've seen, Leslie is quite a beautiful woman. After her husband disappeared, she had a breakdown and my sources tell me she's still institutionalized."

"And she won't let a man near her?" Savannah asked. "So you need a woman to…do what?"

"To see if you can get anything out of her. I don't know how rational she is or how much she knows or remembers, but I need to find out. I figured she might talk to another woman—especially one who is very attractive."

"Well, thank you, Sir." She glanced at Michael before asking Craig, "But what does attractiveness have to do with anything?"

Craig leaned against the back of the sofa. "I'm told that she responds to beautiful women and doesn't seem to have much use for women who aren't pretty. It's some result of her illness, I guess," he explained.

Savannah glanced at Michael before responding to Craig. "Yeah, I'll help if I can. Just give me a list of questions. Who will she think I am? I mean, how will I identify myself?"

"I haven't quite decided. But I'm thinking you could masquerade as a journalist."

"Colbi's a journalist," Michael said. "Why not get her to do it? She's used to it and she's an attractive woman."

"Colbi is a journalist and she's pretty," Craig said, "but I have a hunch that she would relate more closely with Savannah."

"From one to ten, what's the danger level?" Michael asked, his eyes piercing Craig's.

"Uh…gosh, maybe 0 to 1. I mean, Savannah will be driving on the freeway to get there and we all know that driving can be a detriment to our health." He chuckled. "No, Michael, she's not in any danger. The worst that could happen is that Leslie won't talk or can't remember anything."

***

The following afternoon, after getting the go-ahead from Craig, Savannah dropped off Lily at Margaret's and drove forty miles to the facility where Leslie Sparks had lived for the past four years.

Savannah walked into the building at twelve-thirty, sharp. She approached the reception desk. "I'd like to see Sharon Crosley, please. I'm Savannah Ivey."

The receptionist looked Savannah up and down and then said, "Sure." She punched some numbers on the phone pad and said into the receiver, "A Savannah Ivey here to see you." She nodded, hung up the phone, and said, "Go on in—second door on your left."

Savannah thanked the receptionist and walked down the hallway to a door marked *Private*. She was warmly greeted by a short stocky woman with shaggy blond hair framing a friendly, round face. "Sit down, Ms. Ivey."

Once both women were seated, Sharon said, "As you know, I'm Leslie's caseworker, nurse, friend—you name it. She doesn't get many visitors." She sighed. "Well, she did at first, but she turned them all away, so few come to see her anymore."

"Can you tell me who does visit her?" Savannah asked.

"Sure—her twin sister, a long-time childhood friend, and, she surprised me by allowing a new friend in a few weeks ago. Let's see—her name was Julie, I believe."

Savannah perked up. "Julie? What can you tell me about her?"

"What, her personality? Career? Position? Looks?"

"Let's start with looks," Savannah said.

"That's easy, I have a photo." She pulled a file from a drawer on her left. She started to hand Savannah a photo, but then said, "This is not for publication."

"Of course not," Savannah said, reaching for the photo. She took one look at it and handed it back, attempting not to let her emotions show. *That's the dead woman, Julie. My gosh, what business did she have with Leslie?* It took a moment for Savannah to realize Sharon was talking to her.

"So tell me about your mission here today."

"Oh, yes. I'm writing a story about successful women living in institutions and how they manage to survive in a facility such as this one—where seemingly all of their freedom is taken from them."

"Is that what you think…that we take away their freedom?" Sharon snapped.

"No, no. that's not me talking. That's the general consensus. I'm here to shed a more positive light on your program and how women who were successful in business and in life find creative ways to manage in a system like this one." She looked at Sharon. "As I understand it, intelligent, successful women handle their confinement differently than most others. Do you think she'll be receptive to my questions?"

"Now that depends. She has her good days and bad. She's still on a bit of a roller coaster—needs things constant around her, freaks out when things change—but not all the time. On a clear day, you wouldn't know there was a thing wrong with her."

"What about the other days?" Savannah asked.

"Well, let's just hope you've caught her on a good day." Sharon stood. "I saw her this morning and she seemed calm and relatively content." She looked hard at Savannah and said, "I think she'll like meeting you. Come on. I'll take you to her." She said over her shoulder, "I told her you were coming."

Sharon rapped lightly on the door to room 222 and then opened it and peered inside. "Leslie, I brought a new friend," she said. "Okay if I bring her in?"

Savannah didn't hear a reply, but Sharon ushered her in, nonetheless. Once inside, she could see a blond woman dressed in all white, sitting at a large window with her back to her guests. Sharon walked to the left of the woman and addressed her. "Good afternoon, Leslie." She motioned for Savannah to join her. "This is Savannah Ivey. She'd like to visit with you for a while."

Savannah looked down at the woman, who was seated in a small dark-blue print recliner chair staring out the window upon lovely gardens below. "What a beautiful view you have," Savannah said.

Leslie looked up at Savannah through one blue eye. Her other eye was covered by a shock of long blond hair. She smiled. "You're tall."

"Yes, you look as though you're tall, too."

"Five-ten," she said. "And you?"

"Five-nine and a half."

"Sit down, if you want," Leslie said.

Savannah turned a straight chair around and sat in front of Leslie, off to the side a little so as not to spoil her view. Sharon slipped out unnoticed. "You're pretty, too," Leslie said.

"Thank you."

"I used to be pretty." She pulled her hair away from her face and revealed a grotesque scar running the length of her face and across one eye. "Lost my eye when I lost my beauty," she said.

Savannah used every bit of restraint she could muster to keep from reacting. "What happened?" she asked calmly.

"Acid," Leslie said dropping her hair back into place over the scar.

Savannah stared at the woman for a moment. "Is plastic surgery an option?"

"Not for me," she said. "I need to remember what he did. I want *him* to remember what he did. He'll come to see me sometime. He always comes back—he always returns like a male cat to the places he marks and I want him to see what kind of mark he left on me."

"Did your husband do this to you?" Savannah asked, knowing she was way off course where Craig's list of questions was concerned.

Leslie shook her head. "Oh no. He was boring. He was…not very smart. He was dependable, like an old shoe." She stared out the window, as if in another world. "I never liked boring old shoes." She paused. "I should have known better. I should have treasured what I had. I didn't need a new pair of shoes; especially not those shoes…"

"Metaphor?" Savannah said.

"Huh?"

"You're using a metaphor, right?"

Leslie took in a deep breath and then looked over at Savannah. "What's your story? Do you have a boring husband or boyfriend?"

Savannah smiled. "I have an amazing husband and a baby daughter."

Leslie didn't smile. She stared at Savannah and studied her clothes, sparse jewelry, and most of all, her sensible but fashionable shoes. “So you want to know what it’s like in here?”

“Uh, yes. Let me see, I have some questions.” She looked Leslie in the eye and said, “You seem to have adjusted nicely to this…home. Can you tell me if it took some time or have you always found it comfortable?”

Leslie looked at Savannah. Savannah wasn’t sure of her intentions—would she respond or not? Finally she said, “It’s as if I’ve always been here. Yeah, they’re nice to me—don’t make me do anything I don’t want to do. I can sit here and think all day if I want.” She suddenly engaged Savannah, saying, “I’d like it if you’d tell them I’d rather not talk to Dr. James anymore. He makes me think about things I don’t want to think about. I have my own thoughts and I don’t want him telling me what I should think.” She leaned forward toward Savannah and asked, “Do you get what I’m saying?”

“Yes, I think I do,” Savannah said. “Do you remember what happened just prior to your coming here? You were a librarian, weren’t you? You were married. You remember being married, don’t you? You told me a little about your marriage.”

“Damn it!” she hissed. “I told you I don’t want to think about that.”

Savannah stiffened her posture. “I’d like to hear about what frightens you when you think about those days before coming here. Did something happen?”

Leslie took Savannah’s hand. “I’ve told my sister and my other best friend. Now that you are going to be my friend, I can tell you. But I’m not going to tell that Dr. James or even Sharon. She leaned toward Savannah. “I like Sharon. She’s good to me, but she doesn’t understand because she’s not pretty and desirable like you and like me.” As if sharing a secret, she said, "It's a burden being desirable." She looked at Savannah again—patted her hand. "You know what I mean, don't you?"

Savannah, humoring the woman, nodded and said, "Oh yes. It can be a burden."

"So when he came to take me, it was my obligation to go with him. It was my obligation to leave my husband behind. But when it was all over…" Leslie began to cry. "When it was all over, everyone had left me. There's always a prettier girl, Savannah. Remember that. There's always a prettier girl and that's what he found…a prettier girl. I knew that, so I decided to leave him. That's when he disfigured me. He didn't want anyone else to have me, you see. That's how deep his love for me was."

Savannah was about to break the silence that seemed to last forever, when Leslie said, "Julie isn't pretty—not in the way that you are and I am. But she loved him, too. She wanted to know the truth and she came to me for the truth."

By the time Savannah had bid Leslie goodbye, she was shaking. She sat in her car for a full five minutes before she could settle down enough to make a necessary call.

***

An hour later, she walked into a coffee shop in Hammond. She spotted him right away and walked in his direction. "Craig, thank you for meeting me here. My aunt has agreed to keep Lily for another hour because I just had to talk to you."

"What happened, Savannah?" he asked, reaching for one of her hands. "You're shaking. Are you all right?"

"No," she said. "It was a horrifying experience meeting Leslie and listening to her. You were right, by the way. She connected with me almost instantly and decided to confide in me." She rested her elbows on the table. "She has confided in very few people, she says. According to her, she hasn't even told her psychiatrist what caused her breakdown. But she did tell someone we know—someone who…" Savannah took in a ragged breath. "…someone who's now dead! Murdered!"

"Slow down, Savannah. Are you saying that she talked to Julie?"

"Yes."

"When?"

"I checked with Leslie's caseworker. It was a week before Julie was murdered."

Craig sat back in his chair and contemplated this new piece of information.

Savannah began speaking a little more slowly. "I think Leslie was having an affair and either he or she or both of them killed her husband. So the gunman who's been threatening Michael and Damon is probably his killer and maybe her lover—at least he was four years ago." She took a breath to calm herself before saying, "He threw acid in her face, blinded her in one eye, and scarred her face terribly. She thinks he's coming to see her. She has evidently been waiting four years for him to come."

"What makes her think he's coming there?"

"I don't know. For the most part, she's out of touch with reality." Savannah hesitated. "There seemed to be occasional clarity, but..." Savannah shook her head slowly. "That poor, poor woman."

"Did she give you a name, Savannah?"

"No. But let's look at what we know about this guy so far," she suggested. "He's a relentless womanizer, goes for the pretty ones, and is capable of violent acts and maybe even murder."

"What we don't know is if the Chris Sparks murder and Julie's murder were perpetrated by the same person."

"But it makes sense that they were. What if Leslie told Julie the name of the man who killed her husband and Julie used it to blackmail him. He waited for the right moment and killed her, too." Savannah looked down at her hands. "Or he killed her in a rage when she confronted him. But it would have to be someone that both Leslie and Julie knew."

"And he had to have access. I can see your point about motive. But what about opportunity?" Craig asked.

"Craig, a known womanizer is one of your suspects. He used to live here. Auntie knew him and so did Glenda Cathcart, but I don't know her story." Savannah's eyes lit up. "Hey Craig, go talk to Glenda. She must know something or knows someone who does. I'll bet you can get the rest of the story right there at the library. And hurry. Because now that the freezer has been discovered, he might double back and try to silence witnesses from four years ago."

Chapter 9

Later that afternoon, Craig walked into the library. "Hello, Ms. Cathcart. You may recall that we met at the Iveys' house a few weeks ago. I'm Detective Craig Sledge."

She smiled. "Certainly, Detective. How can I help you?"

His demeanor shifted from cordial to serious. "I'm actually here on business. Do you have a few minutes? I'd like to ask you some questions."

"Sure. Let's talk in my office."

Once seated, Craig began, "Ms. Cathcart…"

"Glenda."

"Glenda, do you recall four years ago when Leslie Sparks was librarian? Were you here then?"

"I was assistant librarian across town, brought here just before Leslie…left."

"Do you think she was having an affair?"

Glenda hesitated. "That was the rumor. I can tell you the names of staff who worked here during that rather…tumultuous time. They have a lot of stories." She tightened her lips and then said, "I don't like telling stories out of school, as they say, but…if it helps the innocent, I must say it."

"What's that?" Craig asked.

"Now that that poor man's body has been found…" she lowered her head, "and to think he was in this library all those years…" She shuddered. "Well, I did see something once. I was working odd hours during that period and there was all this construction going on. One man I saw here occasionally during that brief period was that videographer, Lance. He was at Savannah and Michael's party, you know. Good-looking guy. Rumor was that he and Leslie were running around together and we all suspected that he had something to do with her husband's disappearance. And now he's back," she said.

"Did you ever see him with Ms. Sparks?" Craig asked.

She thought about the question. "No, I don't think so. But I saw him with someone else. One night I walked in on him and one of our young volunteers—she couldn't have been more than seventeen…and what was he…like late thirties or something? There they were, wrapped in each other's arms, kissing like the world was coming to an end." She paused. "She was a beauty. I wondered, what her parents would say about it. I was so angry at him for luring her in. Besides, I thought he was Leslie's man-friend." She looked at Craig. "Of course, Leslie was married, but at least she was an adult and capable of making her own decisions."

"What's the girl's name? Do you know where she is now?"

"Yeah, I do. Tiffany works at the ice-cream parlor. She's waiting to be discovered. Wants to be a film star."

Craig made a few notes and then pulled a folded piece of paper from his jacket pocket. "This is a list of library staff and volunteers we spoke to four years ago while investigating the disappearance of Chris Sparks. Can you tell me who still works here; which ones might be high priority witnesses?"

After the librarian commented appropriately, Craig nodded, saying, "Thank you Ms…Glenda. You've been most helpful."

"Do you think he's the murderer, Detective?" she asked.

He thought about the question and said, "We should know that soon enough."

Craig climbed into his unmarked official car and punched a number into his phone. "Cheryl, this is Detective Craig Sledge. Can we talk for a sec?"

"Why? Haven't you harassed me enough?"

"Listen, Cheryl, the right answers just might get you off the hook. The questions this time are not about you. I think you can relax."

There was silence, and then, "I'm listening."

"Cheryl, how long have you and Lance Grayson been a couple?"

"Um, what do you mean by couple?"

"Come on Cheryl. I can't help you if you don't cooperate. And from where I sit, you could be in a whole lot of hot water—up to your neck, in fact."

"Okay, okay, she said with a forced sigh. Yeah, we've been hanging out for about…uh almost a year, on and off."

"Why on and off, may I ask?"

There was more silence. "Two reasons. He strays."

"He does what?"

"Strays, you know, goes looking for greener pasture."

"He's a player?"

"Yeah, pretty much. He likes women and he likes to have a variety pack. But he always comes back to me."

"So you wait?"

"Yeah, sorta."

"Meaning?" Craig asked

"I don't exactly wait-wait. I date—have my own fun."

"But you're there when Grayson comes back."

"Yeah. I hold my options open."

"You said there were two reasons why your relationship is on and off. What's the second?"

"I get tired of being knocked around."

Craig perked up. "He beats you?"

"Oh, I don't think you can say that. He just likes to rough up his chicks—it's his thing, if you know what I mean. I don't take it personally."

"Cheryl, in your opinion, is he capable of murder?"

"Wow, bringing out the big guns, huh, Detective? You know, I really have no reason to protect his butt any longer, so I'm going to tell it like it is. Yes, I know for a fact that he is capable of murder. How's that?" She paused and then said, "And don't ask me how I know because until you get him locked up, my lips are zipped."

"Sounds as though he's threatened you?"

"Something like that. Now am I off the hook for that witch's murder?"

Craig hesitated. "Sure, Cheryl, as long as it wasn't you who did it."

***

The Iveys were having dinner at home when Craig called Michael's cell phone. "Michael, I think you and Savannah ought to take the baby and your animals and spend the night in a motel or at her aunt's or something."

"What!?" Michael shouted.

Savannah looked at him from across the table, fear in her eyes.

"Michael, get out of there. They just found Leslie Sparks strangled and I don't think you're safe. Pack up, decide where you're going. I'm sending a couple of guys over to give you safe passage."

"Will do. Thanks Craig." After ending the call, Michael looked at Savannah. His lips quivered. "Honey, we're evacuating for the night. Go put a few things in a bag for the three of us. I'll call your aunt and tell her we're coming over."

Savannah stood, but didn't move. "What's going on, Michael?"

"I'll explain later. Take Lily and go do as I say, NOW!" She picked up the baby and he carried the cradle swing into the living room. As he started walking down the hallway to get the fold-up portable crib, he heard the sound of a car on the gravel driveway. He pulled the drapes back a little and saw a lone man walking toward the house. Michael could see the glint of something in his hand. *Good Lord,* he thought. *What do I do now?*

He rushed into the bedroom and grabbed the baseball bat he had kept there ever since a stalker had followed Colbi to their home months earlier.

Knock-knock

"Who is it?" Michael asked. He turned on the porch light and peered from behind the drape again. He could see the back of a man wearing a windbreaker-type jacket and a baseball cap. Suddenly the man turned and Michael could see his face. "Damon," he said in relief. He opened the door and pulled him into the house, looking out into the yard quickly before closing the door.

"What's the deal Michael?" he asked. "You expecting someone?"

"I hope not. But Craig has ordered us to leave the house tonight, so I'm not opening the door to anyone I don't know."

"Can I help?" Damon asked.

"Sure can. In fact, with your help, we can take the animals. Savannah's packing for us. I'll get the carriers and you can help me load up the cats."

"Glad to do it."

"Hey, what did you come by for, anyway?" Michael asked as they rushed to the service porch to get the carriers.

He held out Michael's drill. "Just bringing this back. Thanks for letting me borrow it."

"Sure thing. How'd the carpentry work go?" he asked as he took the drill, set it aside, and handed Damon a cat carrier.

Damon took the carrier and grinned. "I don't think I can get my own renovation show on TV yet, but it seems to be a serviceable shelf."

"Walter's on the plum chair in the living room," Michael said. "Can you put him in that carrier?"

"Sure."

Michael deposited two more carriers in the living room and then walked down to the nursery. "How's the packing coming, hon?" He asked when he saw Savannah stuffing things into Lily's diaper bag. He grabbed her around the waist and said, "Ready for an adventure?"

"I guess, but I'm scared."

"Just get us packed. I'm gathering up the animals. I'll meet you in the living room."

"Who's here, Michael? I heard you talking to someone. Or was that my aunt you were talking to."

"Dang, I forgot to call her. I'll do that now." He placed the call and then picked up Buffy with one hand and carried her to Damon. "Can you put her in the small carrier? Then see if you can find Rags. I think he's upstairs." He turned away from Damon and said into his phone, "Oh, hi, Maggie. We have a problem. Craig wants us out of the house. We're on our way over with the menagerie. Can you make room for us? Great, thanks. I'll tell you all about it when we get there. Gotta go, Maggie."

Michael looked up in time to see Damon hurrying down the stairs with Rags in his arms.

He opened the door to the third carrier and Damon pushed him inside.

"Better get their food," Michael said, rushing toward the kitchen. "Oh heck, Maggie and Max have cat food." He headed out. "Not dog food, though," he turned and went back into the kitchen to retrieve Lexie's bowl and food.

Lexie climbed out of her bed, shook herself, and walked over to Michael, ready to be fed.

"No, you had your dinner. This is for later. But we'd better take your bed. Gads, this family requires a lot of stuff," he quipped, trying to keep the mood light.

Once he'd deposited Lexie's belongings next to the cat carriers near the front door, he reached out and shook Damon's hand. "Hey, thanks for the help. Really appreciate it. But I think you should get out of here. Craig thinks it's some sort of danger zone tonight."

Suddenly, the two men noticed headlights shining through the stained glass windows framing the front door. "That's probably our police escort," Michael said. He covertly pulled back an edge of the drape and peered out.

"Is it them?" Damon asked.

"Yeah, I think so. There are two of them and they're coming this way. Oh yeah, it's them. I can see the sheriff's car. Savannah, let's go," he called.

"I need help," she said.

"Of course she does," Michael said. "She has two bags and the baby…" he started down the hall.

"I'll help her," Damon said. "You let the cops in and then we can load the cats in your car."

"Okay. Thanks."

Once the Iveys' SUV was packed with the entire family and their belongings, Damon drove off in his own car. Michael followed him out of the driveway and down the road as far as Margaret's and Max's place, a sheriff escort accompanying them.

When the couple exited the car, Max and Margaret greeted them in the driveway. "What's going on, Michael?" Margaret asked breathlessly.

"Let's get everyone inside and we'll tell you all about it," Michael said. He turned to Deputy Ben. "So will you be watching over us here or watching over our house?"

"Both," he responded. "We know he's out there somewhere and we're pretty sure you're his next mark. So we are looking for him wherever he shows up. We have a bead on his acquaintances here and the car he's driving. He's on the radar of departments in three counties. We *will* get him. As soon as we do, you folks can go home and relax."

"Come on, Savannah," Max said, putting his arm around her and the baby and walking them into the house. He called over to Margaret, "Maggie, take care of her. I'll help Michael."

"Vannie, you're shaking like a leaf," Margaret said when she approached her niece.

"I'm so scared, Auntie. So scared."

"You're safe here. And you heard Ben; they will stay here until he's caught." Once inside, Margaret turned to Savannah and asked, "Who are they looking for, anyway? Michael didn't give me any details on the phone."

"I don't know much yet, either, but I'm pretty sure it's Lance Grayson."

Margaret gasped. "Holy Cow. He's still after you?"

"No, he's after Michael."

"Michael," she said thoughtfully. "I didn't know Lance had changed…persuasions…"

"No, Auntie, he wants to…hurt Michael. Or at least Craig thinks he does. Lance thinks Michael has information that will incriminate him."

"What kind of information?" she asked.

Just then, Max and Michael carried in the three cats. Michael asked, "Where do you want them, Max?"

"Well, we have an empty pen out in the cat house, or they can roam the house with our group. It's up to you."

"Savannah, what do you say we put the cats in the pen tonight—okay with you?"

"Yes, I guess," she said.

"Here's your dog," Deputy Ben said, leading her in by the leash.

"Just drop the leash," Savannah said. "Come here, Lexie." She petted her reassuringly and commanded her to lie down while the men finished unloading the car.

Eight minutes later, Michael and Max joined the women in the living room. Savannah sat on the sofa, cradling Lily in her arms.

"So Michael, what is the rest of the story?" Margaret asked. "Why are you here?"

He sat down next to Savannah and took her hand. After clearing his throat, he said, "They think Lance Grayson killed Chris Sparks and Julie." He squeezed Savannah's hand. "Today, they found Leslie Sparks strangled to death in her room at the institution."

Savannah gasped. "Oh no," she said.

Michael continued, "Someone there identified Grayson. Now they think he's after me."

"Good gosh," Max said. "That videographer?"

"That womanizer?" Maggie said, anger apparent in her voice.

"That poor woman," Savannah said. "She was sure he would come back, but I don't think she thought he would kill her."

Everyone looked at Savannah. She continued talking quietly in monotone, "She was waiting for him. All those years, she waited."

"Honey, are you okay?" Michael asked.

"Oh Michael," she said, bursting into tears, "she waited four years with that disfigured face and he finally came…and he killed her?" she asked, shaking her head.

Margaret reached over and took sleeping baby Lily. Michael folded Savannah into his arms and rocked her while she sobbed.

An hour later, Michael emerged from the spare bedroom. "My girls are sleeping soundly," he announced to Margaret and Max, who were both sitting in their recliner chairs reading. Layla, Margaret's tangerine faux Persian lay next to her on the leg rest. Two additional cats were curled up in kitty beds here and there and Lexie looked comfy in her favorite bed.

"Wait, do you hear that?" Michael said.

"What?" Margaret asked, her dark-brown eyes wide, her brows disappearing under her bangs.

"Sirens," Max said. "Yeah, I hear them."

"They're getting closer. Do you think they're coming out here?" she asked.

"I just hope they don't wake Savannah," Michael said.

Margaret looked toward the hallway. "Too late," she said.

Everyone turned and saw Savannah walking into the living room carrying Lily wrapped in a blanket.

"Did she wake up? I'm sorry, I didn't hear her," Michael said.

"No, she didn't. I just couldn't leave her there out of my sight. I heard the sirens. Are they going to our house?"

"Maybe we should have gone to Iris's," Michael said.

"She doesn't have room for all of you," Margaret said. "You'll be safe here."

"Michael, walk out with me to the pens to check on the cats, will you?" Savannah said.

"Um, okay, I guess it's safe."

"Yeah, you don't have to go outside," Max said. "Just take that side door and you'll walk right into the cat house."

"They don't look too upset," Savannah said upon seeing the three cats. "I might take Buffy back with me, though. She would be more comfortable near Lily, don't you think?"

"Whatever you say, hon. Sure, let's take her and her bed in the house and see how she does."

"Michael, the sirens are coming here. My gosh, they're close. Let's get back in the house."

"Look, guys," Margaret said, from her living room window. "Your house is all lit up."

"It's not on fire, is it?" Savannah asked, fear in her voice.

"No, car lights and spotlights. They must think he's lurking around over there." She turned to Savannah and Michael. "I'm so glad you came over here. Craig really had your back." She hugged Savannah and the baby in her arms and started to cry.

Bang! Bang!

Bark! Bark! Bark!

"Settle, Lexie," Michael said, gently petting the dog's head.

"Dear God," Max said. "Let's go to the center of the house—the hallway. Hurry," he said, herding the two women in that direction.

"Oh no," Savannah said.

"What?" Margaret asked.

"They woke up the baby."

Savannah moved to the back of the small hallway and began bouncing and walking a little in an attempt to calm the baby. "Let me take her," Michael said.

Savannah handed her to him. "Now stay back here away from the front of the house!" she said sounding near hysterics.

Margaret looked over at her niece and rubbed her arm with her hand. "You know, kiddo, I've seen you in several seriously dangerous situations and I've never seen you so upset."

"You've never seen anyone threaten my baby. It's not just about me, anymore, you know. I have Lily to think about and Michael," she wailed.

Max walked up to Savannah and hugged her. "We'll be okay. Don't you worry."

"Thanks Max. You're a rock," Savannah said. She smiled up at him through tears and patted the hand that hugged her shoulder.

"My phone," Michael said. "Who would be calling in the middle of a shootout?" He looked at the screen and announced, "It's Craig." Into the phone, he said, "Craig. What's going on?"

"Lance Grayson is on his way to the morgue."

"Thank God," Michael said, releasing what felt like an enormous amount of tension in one giant sigh. He said out loud to the others, "They got him." He then asked Craig, "So was that you guys shooting outside here?"

"Yeah. You're at Maggie's, are you?"

"Yes."

"Well, he showed up here at your house and our guys confronted him. He pulled out a gun. When he wouldn't drop it, the officers responded by firing. He won't be hurting anyone else in this lifetime."

"Thanks, Craig. Thanks so much."

"Doin' my job. That's all." His demeanor changed when he asked, "How's Savannah?"

"Pretty shook up. But she'll be fine now that you've taken care of the threat."

"Tell her, I still think she and her cat make a good detective team. 'Night Michael."

Michael tucked his phone away and looked around at everyone. "Well, we can go home, now. It's safe." When no one spoke, he said, "Or, I guess we can have a…what do you call those sleep parties?"

"Sleepover," Savannah said quietly, a hint of a smile emerging through tears.

"Slumber party," Margaret said. "Yes! Spend the night. Max and I would love the company." She addressed her husband. "Imagine, Max, waking up to Lily's sweet smile in the morning."

"Yeah, that would be a treat," he said.

"Well, what do you say, Savannah?" Michael asked. "You and Lily are already in your jammies."

"I guess so. I would like to go to bed in a house full of family tonight. Only…"

"Only what, Vannie?"

"Only, I miss Rags."

"What?" Margaret said. "He's about five steps from you. What do you mean you miss him?"

"He likes to put me to bed. And I miss him."

Michael smiled. "She's right, guy. Rags almost always follows Savannah into the bedroom at bedtime. Once she's tucked in, he may stay or he may leave for the night."

"Awww, we can't separate the slumber-twins, can we?" Margaret said. "I'll go get Rags."

She turned and said, “But I can’t bring Rags in without Walter. He probably misses his best friend, Lexie.”

“Probably,” Michael said. He smiled over at Savannah, who still stood in the hallway. “It looks like everyone has somebody in this household tonight.”

***

“Good morning, honey,” Michael said snuggling up against his wife.

“G’ mornin’,” she said stretching and yawning. Suddenly she sat up and looked around. “Oh, I forgot,” she said lying back down, “we’re at Auntie’s.” She raised up again and said, “Lily! Where’s Lily? Her bed’s empty!”

Michael lifted himself up and looked over at the portable crib. “Well, she didn’t crawl away. She must be with Maggie.”

Savannah leaped out of bed and rushed through the open door, down the hall, and through her aunt’s living room. “Auntie?” she called. When she entered the kitchen, she stopped and took in a welcome breath. There, all smiles, sitting on Margaret’s lap, was Lily, hugging her calico kitty to her chest with both pudgy hands. Max sat on a stool on the other side of the room waving a feather wand across the floor, engaging a couple of young cats in play. The baby laughed each time one of them ran, jumped, or scooted across the floor. Buffy and Layla sat on the kitchen table watching the activity.

“Just go back to bed, you, two,” Margaret said when she saw Michael join Savannah at the kitchen door. “We have everything under control, right Max?”

“Sure do,” he said smiling.

"I didn't even hear you come in," Savannah said. "Was she fussing?"

"Just started. I grabbed her before she woke you up."

Max chuckled. "Yeah, she stood in the hallway for an hour waiting for the baby to make a sound."

"Did not," she said, defensively.

Savannah walked toward the baby, bent down, and kissed her cheek. "Well, I'm ready to get up. Want me to fix breakfast for us?" she asked.

"It's under control," Max said. "I made a breakfast casserole. I'll put it in the oven as soon as you're ready to eat."

"Cool," Michael said. He moved closer to the window and peered out toward their house. "Everything looks okay. I'll be glad to get home," he said. He turned toward Margaret and Max. "Not that this hasn't been fun. Sure do appreciate you guys being here," he said.

"Yes, we do," Savannah agreed. She then said, "I'm going to get a quick shower."

"So breakfast in, what…" Max asked, "…an hour?"

"Naw, she's pretty speedy," Michael said. He studied his watch. "I'd say she'll be ready for her juice and coffee in seven minutes flat."

Margaret raised her eyebrows. "Really?"

"Yup," he said. "Now get going, hon, you're being timed."

Six minutes and fifty-four seconds later, Savannah emerged dressed, smiling, and with her wet hair in a side braid. "Well, I'll be; she did it," Max said. "You must be a unique woman. It's been my experience that women spend a lot of time in the bathroom."

"Oh, I can do that, too, when I want," Savannah said. "But this morning, I'm hungry. Is that casserole ready yet?"

"Oh, my phone. It's Craig," Michael announced. He walked out into the cat room to take the call. When he returned, Savannah was pouring juice and coffee, Max was just taking the casserole out of the oven, and Margaret was playing peek-a-boo with Lily.

"Anything new?" Savannah asked when she saw Michael step back into the kitchen.

He shook his head. "Not much. Craig wants to come over this morning and look around in case there's something they missed last night. He still has some puzzles to solve."

"Are you going to work today?" Savannah asked.

"Naw, I asked Bud if he could handle things today. I told him I'm needed by my family."

Savannah reached out and caressed his neck for a moment. "Always," she said.

"So what puzzles does Craig want to solve?" Max asked.

"Like, how did Grayson get the heavy freezer out of that basement room and down the ravine," Michael said.

"Yeah, how in the heck did he get it up those stairs?" Margaret asked.

"I suggested that maybe he paid a couple of strong teenagers or homeless guys to help him."

"Sure, that makes sense," Max said.

Michael continued, "I told him a lot of young boys have trucks these days, so Grayson might have put gas in a truck in exchange for some kids driving up into the canyon and dumping it."

Max nodded. “Good thinking, Michael.”

Margaret placed Lily in her cradle swing and then said, “So the sunken room did hide a mystery. I guess the reason the room was closed up was actually to hide the body, huh?”

“That’s what Craig figures,” Michael said. “But he says you can’t solve a murder by assumption.”

Margaret scrunched up her face. “What does that mean?”

“He doesn’t think Lance Grayson murdered Chris Sparks?” Max asked.

“He’s pretty sure he did, but I don’t think he has evidence. Just like he doesn’t have conclusive evidence in Julie’s murder,” Michael explained. “I guess he didn’t get a confession from Grayson before he died.”

***

The Iveys arrived home later that morning. After putting Lily down for a nap, Savannah joined Michael on the wrap-around porch. She set the baby monitor on the railing and picked up a section of the newspaper Michael was reading. Just then she noticed Rags looking at them from the kitty perch at the kitchen window. “Oh Ragsy,” she said, “do you want to come outside?” She spoke to Michael. “It is a pretty day; I think I’ll bring him out.”

Michael smiled. “Sure, he’ll enjoy that.” He peered over the paper at her and said, “But make sure you leave his leash on this time. I don’t feel like climbing any trees today.”

Savannah led the lanky cat out the door on his long tether and then let him take the lead.

“Where’s he taking you?” Michael asked with a chuckle.

"I don't know," she said. "I think we're going to the corral."

Just then, Savannah heard a car approaching the house. She squinted in the direction of the driveway and called out to Michael, "I think Craig's here." She then waved and hollered, "Hi Craig! We're out here!"

"Good morning," Craig said as he walked toward her. "Is he taking you for a walk?" he asked, grinning down at the cat.

"Yes. So how are you this morning?" she asked. "You had quite a night, didn't you?"

"Sure did."

"And you came back to look for clues?" she asked. "You don't have conclusive evidence that Lance killed anyone yet?"

"It's starting to come together," he said. Just then he noticed Michael walking toward them. "Hi guy," he said. "You were right about Grayson's accomplices."

"Huh?" Michael said.

"I found a couple of the homeless who hang out on the west side near the library. When I told them Grayson was dead, they had no problem spilling their guts about helping him dispose of that freezer. Of course, they didn't know what was in it. They ID'd Grayson. We may never have the evidence we need to tie that case up in a pretty bow, but the circumstantial is awfully strong."

"Gosh, what type of evidence do you need, Craig," Savannah asked, "a confession?"

"Pretty much."

Michael scratched his head. "Did you find out how he got into the library?"

"No," Craig said. He looked beyond Michael toward the tack room. "Is that your jacket, Michael? Your cat's messing with it."

Michael looked up. "No, not mine. Is it yours, Savannah?"

She spun around. "No." She walked toward the cat and picked up the light-blue windbreaker off the ground. "It looks familiar," she said. Just then something fell from the jacket. "Keys," she exclaimed.

She started to pick them up when Craig said, "Wait." He walked over to the keys, lifted them with a pen, and examined them.

Suddenly Savannah shouted, her voice a few octaves higher than normal, "Lance! He wore a jacket like this the day of the party!"

Craig carefully slipped the keys into a small evidence bag and tucked it into his jacket pocket. "He must have taken it off when he became aware of us last night. He had a dark flannel shirt on when we found him. He shed this jacket probably so he wouldn't be easy to spot. That creep actually thought he could get away from us," he said with a snicker.

"You always get your man—or woman—is that it, Craig?" Michael said.

"Pretty much," Craig said. He patted his pocket and said, "What do you want to bet the library key is on this ring?"

"So you think he kept it all these years?" Michael asked.

"Yeah. Wouldn't you, if you'd left a body there in a freezer? He had to know it would be discovered at some point and that he'd have to go to plan B."

"And he'd need the key in order to execute plan B, right?" Savannah said. "Craig, do you know where he lived?"

"Yeah, while here in this area, he bunked with a young gal in Straley. I hear that she works as a receptionist for a doctor's office there." He pulled his notepad from his pocket and flipped through the pages. "A Dr. B. Jordan on Hart Street. I plan to go talk to him this afternoon."

Savannah exclaimed. "Craig, that's not a him, that's my sister!"

"What?" he said.

"Dr. Brianna Jordan is my sister. You know my sister."

"Yeah, but, I guess I didn't remember her last name. Well, I'll be. So do you know her receptionist, Monica?"

"Sure, I've met her. She was dating Lance Grayson? Good grief, she's only a kid—maybe twenty."

"Twenty-four," Craig said.

"That's disgraceful. He was more perverted than I thought," Savannah said in disgust.

"He was a piece of work, all right," Craig agreed. He scanned the yard and said, "Well, I'd better look around and then I have to head over to Straley." He pointed at Rags. "I think your cat is ready to get some exercise, there."

Savannah looked at Rags. "Yeah, he seems a little antsy. I'd better go walk with him."

"Okay, see you guys later," Craig said. He patted his jacket pocket and added with a chuckle, "Thanks for the evidence, Deputy Rags. Good work."

***

"Vannie, we've been robbed!"

"What? Oh, Auntie, how? When? What did they take?"

"I don't know for sure. The only thing I've found missing so far is one of my diamond earrings—you know those sweet teardrops Max gave me for our anniversary," Margaret said. "One of them is gone. I'm just sick."

"Have you looked everywhere?" Savannah asked.

"Yes, everywhere. It's gone, I tell you. Gone!"

"Don't give up hope, Auntie," Savannah said. "I lost a bracelet once. Couldn't find it for weeks. Finally, it showed up when I moved my dresser out to clean. I'd looked under there, felt all over underneath the dresser, and came up with nothing. When I pulled it out weeks later, there it was, hiding in the crook of the dresser leg."

"Okay, I'll keep looking, but what if I vacuumed it up or picked it up with cat hair and it's at the Hammond dump?" Margaret wailed.

"Want me to come over and help?" Savannah offered.

Margaret paused, then said into the phone, "No. I'll keep watching for it. You're probably right. It's here somewhere; I just haven't looked in the right place yet." She took a breath and then asked, "So what are you two doing today?"

"I took Rags out for a walk earlier. Lily is up from her nap and I was just thinking about what to fix for dinner."

"You sound so domesticated. Well, enjoy. I'll talk to you later."

"Okay, good bye," Savannah said before ending the call. So what are we going to fix Daddy for supper?" she asked in the baby's direction. Just then, her cell phone rang again.

"Oh hi, Craig," she said into the phone. "What did you find out in Straley?"

"Not much. I met Monica, but she didn't have much to say. She sure was upset when I told her Grayson was dead. In fact, she was too distraught to be questioned. She even had to leave work. I offered to drive her home—I really wanted to look around at her place—but she declined. Guess I'll have to get a search warrant."

"Gosh, that poor girl. Sounds like she really had it bad for that jerk. It's probably best that he's out of her life."

"That's what I'm thinkin'."

Brring, brring.

"Oh Craig, my house phone's ringing. I'd better get it. Can I call you back?"

"No need. Just wanted to catch you up to date. 'Bye, Savannah."

"Hello?"

"Hi Vannie, it's your sister."

"Well, hi. Whatcha doing?"

"Just leaving the office. Hey, I'm headed your way. I wondered if I could borrow your rug shampooer. Now that Frankie is past his baby kitten stage, I want to clean the carpet here at my apartment."

"I thought Frankie and his mom lived at Bud's ranch."

"Yeah, but I miss him when I come back to Straley, so I take him home with me most weeks. He's gotten to where he enjoys car rides."

"Cool. I'd love to see him...and you. Yes, come on by."

An hour and a half later, Savannah heard the sharp toot of a car horn in front of her house and she hurried to greet her sister. She swung the front door open and noticed that Brianna was not alone. Savannah watched as a young woman climbed out of the passenger side holding a half-grown white kitten who was wearing a harness attached to a leash. "Savannah, you remember Monica," Brianna said, as the two women approached the house.

"Hi," Savannah said. She then reached out and scratched the cat's neck. "Hi Frankie, you cutie patootie."

Monica smiled weakly; looked down at the cat.

"She had a rough time of it today," Brianna said. "I talked her into coming to the ranch with me this evening. She loves animals."

"I can see that," Savannah said. "Come on in. Rags will enjoy seeing Frankie, I'm sure."

As they stepped inside, Brianna spotted Lily in her cradle swing and exclaimed, "There's my precious niece." She knelt down next to the baby. "Look how big you're getting, and pretty. Yes, you're prettier every time I see you…yes you are…" she said. She turned toward Savannah. "Can I pick her up?"

"Sure. She'd love it." She then said, "So you're going to shampoo your carpets, huh?"

"Yeah. Your machine's smaller and easier to use than those you rent from the hardware store."

"Isn't that the truth?" Savannah said. "Works pretty good, too."

"Monica, you can put Frankie down, if you want. Oh, here comes Rags."

"Wow, what an awesome cat," Monica said, squatting and reaching in his direction enticingly.

Rags walked up to her and butted her hand with his head and then rubbed one side of his body against her, knocking her off balance.

"And he's strong," she said, catching herself before falling over.

"Yes, he is," Savannah agreed. "Ragsy, Frankie came to see you," she said to the cat. "Wanna play with Frankie?" She reached down and unsnapped the leash from the harness and the kitten rushed up to Rags and rubbed his body against him.

He then spotted the staircase and raced up the steps, Rags on his tail.

"Well sit down," Savannah invited. "Can I get you something to drink?"

"Do you have bottled water?" Brianna asked.

"Sure," Savannah said. "Monica, would you like water, lemonade, iced tea?"

"Water's fine," she said. "Thanks."

"This is a great house," Monica said, when Savannah returned. "I used to live in a house kind of like this as a kid. I have nice memories of that time."

"Yeah," Brianna said, "Savannah and I have childhood memories of this house, too. My sister and her husband bought it from our aunt."

"Cool," Monica said.

"So how's your job going, Monica?" Savannah asked. She grinned impishly at her sister before asking the younger woman, "Is she a good boss?"

Monica smiled. "The best."

"Of course, you have to say that while she's sitting right here," Savannah joked.

"No, I really mean it. She's more than a boss to me—she's sorta like a mother."

Briana grimaced. "Well, I would have said *friend.* I'm not old enough to be your mother, am I?"

"Naw, but I don't know much about my mother, so it's nice to think of you in that way."

"Monica was adopted," Brianna said, when she saw Savannah look at Monica inquisitively.

"Were you raised here in the area?" Savannah asked.

"Yes, part of the time. My dad, John Bloom, was an attorney in the next county."

"So you had a nice upbringing?" Savannah asked. "You were pleased with your adoptive parents?"

"Yes, I do okay," she said pulling her shoulder-length hair back into a knot. *Pretty face,* Savannah thought. *There's something familiar about her. Maybe it's because I've met her before.*

"Here come the rowdies," Brianna said. "Frankie's having such a good time. Maybe I should get him a kitty playmate. He loves company."

"You've got a good kitty there, Bri," Savannah said. "I don't know if I'd push it."

"Yeah, you're probably right," she agreed. "He is a good boy. I might get a cat like…Rags. Then what would I do?"

"What's wrong with Rags?" Savannah asked, expressing hurt feelings.

"Oh gosh, where do I start?"

"You love Rags. You used to enjoy hanging out with him when I lived in the city."

"Yeah, he kept me entertained, that's for sure," Brianna said. "He's one energetic fellow." She turned toward Monica and said, "You know, we should get going over to Bud's. His mom's making a tamale pie for us."

"Are you staying over?" Savannah asked.

"No, not on a workday night. We'll eat, visit, and head home, right Monica?"

"That's about the size of it," she said, looking a little melancholy.

Once the women had left with the white cat and the rug shampooer, Savannah carried Lily and her cradle swing into the kitchen and started putting a salad together. She smiled over at her daughter and started singing, "This is the way we chop our lettuce, chop our lettuce, chop our lettuce, this is the way we slice our tomatoes and shake, shake, shake our salad dressing."

When Michael walked in, Lily was watching Savannah with interest.

"Oh, I didn't hear you come in," Savannah said.

"Obviously," he said laughing.

"What's that you've got?" she asked.

"I don't know. Found it sticking out from under the throw rug under the coffee table. Looks like a letter. It's not yours?"

Savannah looked at it more closely. "I don't think so. Who's it addressed to?"

Michael turned the envelope over and said, "Monica Bloom."

Savannah faced her husband. "Monica? Let me see that," she said. She looked at the return address, "Grayson." She made a face and said in disgust, "This must be from Lance."

Michael looked confused. "Do you mean your sister's receptionist—that Monica?"

Savannah nodded.

He scratched his head. "But how…?" he started.

"Well, Bri came by a little while ago with Monica and Rags must have…"

"Oh no, not Rags again. Will it ever end?"

Savannah put her hands on her hips. "Will Walter ever stop playing with Lexie? Will Buffy stop being cute? No, it's in their DNA. It's who they are. Rags is a klepto and that's not going to change," she snapped.

"Well okay, then," he said with a chuckle. He turned serious. "I think you'd better turn that over to Craig or give it back to this Monica. It's not your business, Savannah."

She picked up her phone. "Hmm, to call Bri or to call Craig…I just don't know." Before she could decide, her phone rang. "Oh hello Craig, you just helped me make a difficult decision."

"What is it, Savannah?"

"Well, Monica Bloom was just here and Rags…"

Craig began to chuckle. "Don't tell me…"

"Yes, you probably guessed it. He found something and hid it. Michael just discovered it."

"What is it?"

"A letter to Monica from someone named Grayson. I'm assuming it's Lance."

"Wow!" he said. "Now *I* have a decision to make. Do I read the private letter or not?"

"It's been opened already," she said.

He hesitated before saying, "Oh hell, I'll be right over, Savannah…if it's okay with you."

"Sure, we'll be here."

After hanging up, Savannah went back to preparing dinner. Before she could explain to Michael what she knew about Monica, her phone rang again. "Oh hello Auntie," she said. "What's up?"

"Well," Margaret said, laughing, "I have something to tell you."

"What?" she asked.

"I found my earring."

"Oh good news. Where?"

"You're not going to believe it."

"At the dump?"

"No."

"In the shower drain?"

"No. You'll never guess, so you might as well give up."

"Then where?" Savannah asked.

"The litter box?"

"What? One of the cats swallowed it and…"

"No, nothing like that. It was clean, if you know what I mean. It was just buried in the litter box in the back room."

"How do you think it got there?" Savannah asked. "One of your cats…"

"I don't think so. I think it was one of *your* cats."

"Oh no," Savannah cried. "Rags?"

"Who else?" Margaret said.

"Well, I'll be. That's a first—at least I think so." She thought for a moment and said, "Maybe I'd better pay closer attention to what comes out of our cats' litter boxes." She sighed deeply. "Maybe Michael's right. He really is getting to be a pain. But he's my pain and I do love him."

She heard the doorbell and saw Michael head toward the front door. "Hey Auntie, speaking of Rags, he found something today that Craig wants to see. He's here now. Gotta go."

Once the trio was seated around the kitchen table with bottles of water in front of them, Craig asked Savannah, "So how is it that Monica Bloom was here today?"

"Bri brought her by. As you know, she'd had a rough day and my sister wanted to offer a distraction. Apparently, she likes animals and Bri thought she'd enjoy seeing Bud's parents' ranch."

Craig stared at her as if in thought. "Uh-huh," he muttered. He picked up the envelope and turned it over a time or two. He then reached into it and pulled out the letter.

"A long one," he said. He stared down at the letter for a few minutes while Michael and Savannah watched.

Finally Savannah said, "Well?"

Craig looked up at her and then glanced in Michael's direction, "Lance was her father," he said weakly.

"Her what?" Savannah asked.

"Her father," he said more clearly. Evidently, she was adopted when she was still a baby. Grayson is her biological father and he just came into her life a few years ago."

"Where's her mother?" Michael asked.

Craig cleared his throat and straightened his posture. "It seems that she's still around—hiding in plain sight, as they say."

Savannah frowned. "What does that mean, Craig?"

He shook his head. "It's hard to believe, guys, but you know that wrinkled woman who drives that decorated golf cart around?"

"Oh gosh, yes," Savannah said. "I see her in town a lot. I spoke with her at the library the day we were filming. She even pulled into our driveway once."

"When was that?" Craig asked.

"Oh, one day when the film crew was here, actually. I saw her drive that gaudy cart in, stop and look around, and then she left. You know, there's something wrong with her."

"It's called alcohol and drugs," Craig said. "Her name's Kathleen Eckhart. We know her well at the station."

"So what does she have to do with this Monica?" Michael asked.

"Kathleen's evidently Monica's mother."

Savannah's jaw dropped in disbelief. "That woman and Lance?" She thought about it for a moment and said, "Yeah, I can imagine that she was pretty when she was younger…before…"

"Yeah, she was," Craig said. "I saw a picture of her once holding a baby, as a matter of fact. She was a knockout."

"Shocking," Savannah said. "So what else is in the letter?"

"Grayson mentions a package. He says he's sending it to Monica and she's supposed to keep it safe until he comes for it."

"Wow, I wonder what that's all about," Savannah said.

Craig pursed his lips. "That's what I hope to find out, and soon." He looked up at the couple. "By the way, Grayson did have a key to the library on that key ring your cat found."

"You expected as much, didn't you, Craig?" Michael said.

"Yeah. Hey, I see you're about to have dinner. Let me get out of your way so you can proceed with your evening of relaxation."

"Will you get to relax this evening, Craig?" Savannah asked.

"Actually, I believe so. I can't see Monica Bloom until tomorrow, anyway, so I think I'll crash for a while at Iris's before calling it a night."

***

Two nights later, the Iveys shared the front page of the newspaper as they both read the story Damon had written about the updates in the recent murder cases. "So Monica handed over the package to authorities," Michael said. "Good girl."

"Oh, the package Lance sent to her before he died?" Savannah said. She looked down at her hands. "That poor girl. She's a sweet thing. Seems to have her head on straight and her heart in the right place. And to have so much rejection in her life—must be awful."

"I guess she knows who her mother is now, right?" Michael said.

"Yes, it seems so. But what good will it do her to have a mother who doesn't want her and who is a total druggy-alcoholic or mentally ill? Her father's dead. I hope those Blooms who adopted her are nice people and still love her," Savannah said.

"Yeah, she knows her father is a killer, now, too. The package he gave her was supposed to be opened upon his death and evidently, he didn't want to die without confessing everything to her."

Savannah said, "Even Julie's murder. It appears that Craig has his case closure."
She looked pensive, "I guess Lance did love his daughter in his way."

"Yes, if it was convenient at the moment," Michael said. He spoke more sternly, "That's not love, Savannah."

"Yeah, you're right. But it's all he knew."

"Oh, my phone," Savannah said, putting it up to her ear. "Hi Bonnie. How are you, girl?" Savannah looked at Michael and said into the phone, "Well sure. That would be okay. Is there a problem?" Savannah listened to the voice on the other end of the phone for a few minutes and then the pair ended the call. Savannah placed the phone on the coffee table in front of her and stared at it.

"What is it, hon?" Michael asked, concern in his voice. After a few seconds, he said, "Savannah?"

"Oh, sorry. I was just thinking."

"So what did Bonnie say?"

"She wants to bring Peaches home tomorrow."

"That's okay, isn't it?" he asked.

She perked up. "Oh yes. I'm ready to have my mare home—more than ready. I miss her. No, that isn't the problem. The problem is, someone is harassing Bonnie and her husband. They're stealing animals from their place or helping them escape. Several animals have come up missing." She turned toward Michael. "You haven't heard of anyone else missing livestock, have you?"

He shook his head. "No, I sure haven't. Has she? Does she know of others who have lost animals?"

"Well, she thinks she's being singled out—that it's a race issue or maybe there's a disgruntled horse owner who isn't winning ribbons with the horse Bonnie trained…something like that. She doesn't have a clue as to who it would be, though. She wants to tell me more about it tomorrow, in case there's anything I might suggest."

Michael squinted his eyes. "Who does she think you are, Angela Lansbury?"

"No," Savannah said rather indignantly. "I think she just considers me a friend and someone who isn't exactly dense and she'd like to bounce a few ideas off me and get my opinion. Is that okay with you, Mr. Cynical?"

"Whoa there," Michael said, holding his hands out in front of himself defensively. "I was just funnin' you. Of course, you're a friend and a smart one, at that. She's lucky to have you. But…"

"But what?" she asked rather curtly.

"Are you sure you want to be involved in another mystery so soon?"

Savannah studied her husband for a moment before saying, "Bonnie needs me. Tomorrow, I'll let her know I'll be there for her." She cringed. "Gads, I hope I'm not setting myself up to get involved in a gnarly rustling ring."

Michael picked up her hand and squeezed it. "Yeah, me too. Me too."

Made in the USA
Middletown, DE
17 September 2017